MW01610595

A TRUCKER GIRL'S
Dream

By Angel Power

 FriesenPress

Suite 300 - 990 Fort St
Victoria, BC, V8V 3K2
Canada

www.friesenpress.com

Copyright © 2020 by Angel Power
First Edition — 2020

All rights reserved.

No part of this publication may be reproduced in any form, or by any means, electronic or mechanical, including photocopying, recording, or any information browsing, storage, or retrieval system, without permission in writing from FriesenPress.

This is a work of fiction. Names, characters, places and incidents either are the product of the author's imagination or are used fictitiously. Any resemblance to actual persons, living or dead, events, or locales is entirely coincidental.

ISBN
978-1-5255-7968-4 (Hardcover)
978-1-5255-7969-1 (Paperback)
978-1-5255-7970-7 (eBook)

Fiction, Feminist

Distributed to the trade by The Ingram Book Company

CONTENTS

DEDICATION

To Cowboy, who taught me dreams can
And really do come true

Love you always

CHAPTER 1

Take the Risk
or Lose the Chance

It was a beautiful day on the road, and Ruth was looking forward to stopping as the road sign for one of her favourite truck stops came into view. She signalled and took the off ramp to the stop sign. She had been stopping here for as long as she could remember to eat and refuel.

She steered her Chevy half-ton truck into the parking lot. As she opened the door and stepped out, she heard the hiss of semi-trailer air brakes come on. It was a sound she never grew tired of hearing. Ruth had always liked big trucks. She had spent her childhood years hanging out with her father and Bob at LJM Transport along the south shore of Nova Scotia. That was over fifty years ago.

She'd never had the opportunity to travel far in one, but the dream of driving and living the life of a long-haul truck driver had never died. As a wedding present, Bob had given her a little Matchbox tractor and trailer with a note inside the trailer that read, "Never give up on your dream." The little truck sat on her dining room windowsill.

She looked at it every day when she was home. The call of the road had been there ever since she could remember. She travelled extensively with work now, and the life of being a true trucker was still a dream.

Over the years, she had met many truckers who had offered to take her on a trip, but all the offers had fallen by the wayside. Nonetheless, she continued to stop and utilize truck stop services whenever she could. If she could not be a true trucker, she could imagine herself being one every time she stopped. She loved sitting in the diners and overhearing truckers tell stories of the road. They complained about dispatch, and talked about what they were hauling, things they had witnessed, and where they were headed.

She sat talking to waitresses and listened to them describe those who came in on a regular basis. She watched their eyes cloud over and grow misty when they spoke of the ones who had tragically lost their lives in accidents. It was a hard life, but it still held a wanderlust for her.

Today was like any other day for Ruth as she entered the diner. She was coming from booking the last show of a national tour. The parking lot was full of cars, and she knew the place would be full of summer tourists. When she entered, there was a lineup of men, women, and children waiting to be seated at a table. Ruth overheard a waitress say, "It will be at least thirty minutes for a seat."

Ruth stepped forward and peeked around the corner to look at the trucker counter. It was a single-stool, sit-down counter for the truckers, so they could get in, eat, and get out without having to wait in line. There were only two truckers sitting there. She motioned to the waitress, "Would it be okay if I sat at the counter? I am alone, and I only want breakfast."

"Sure, dear, go ahead. I will be with you in a minute."

Ruth walked over and sat down. The waitress came over poured her coffee and took her breakfast order. She sat scrolling through her phone, checking her emails, keeping her head down. As she sipped her coffee, her mind began to wander.

It had been a little over a year since her separation, and at fifty-eight years old, her children were grown and living on their own. Abby was working and living in England, and Ambrose was living not far from where Ruth lived and had returned to school following his divorce.

Ruth worked and travelled in the entertainment industry. It was a great job, and she loved it. It kept her on the road, which was the best part about it. She thought about the past eight years. Her career had taken off when she decided to become Event Coordinator for a national tour. She had been on the road with the musicians almost nonstop. It was exciting, fun, and she had learned so much about the entertainment industry.

When she started, she did not have a clue what she was doing. It did not take long for her to catch on, and the tour she designed took off. She was amazed at how her life had changed while working with the tour. The celebrities she had had the pleasure of meeting and working with had spotless reputations. Names in the industry she could only dream of wanted to work with her on the tour. After three very successful seasons, people were talking about how quickly she had excelled at putting tours together.

She was proud of what she had done. There had been a lot lacking in her life since she had been on her own. Her continuous travelling had come at the cost of her marriage, and she knew at the end there was nothing left to hold on to. Leaving her marriage was a decision a long time in the making, and when she pulled out of the driveway, she vowed never to look back.

Since then, she had dated and had coffee with numerous prospects. The feelings for a serious relationship had never materialized. She was quite content alone, burying herself in work, travelling, and living from hotel to hotel. She had given up on finding a partner and was happy sitting alone at the counter sipping coffee, waiting for her breakfast to arrive.

It was not long before her train of thought was broken by the plate of eggs, bacon, hash browns, and toast that materialized in front of her. The waitress refilled her coffee cup, and Ruth concentrated on eating as her stomach made a little growl of satisfaction.

As she started to eat, a shadow blocked the light from the window. She overheard a male voice, "Do you mind if I sit here?" He motioned to the stool beside her. "I don't bite and I see you already have your breakfast, so I don't think you will."

Looking up, Ruth said with a smile, "Sure, go ahead; sit down," and went back to eating. The man sat on the stool next to her and made himself busy looking at the menu and chatting with the waitress. You could tell he was a regular, and it seemed everyone knew him. He ordered his breakfast, and once again he broke the silence in which Ruth had surrounded herself.

"Who do you truck for?" he asked.

Ruth turned, "I don't truck for anyone. Although, I should." She started to explain what she did for a living and watched as the man listened intently to her words. "What about you? Who do you work for?"

"I work for R.A.E. Trucking hauling oversized and heavy-haul loads."

Ruth listened and detected a strong accent. "Where are you from?"

"Newfoundland. I'm on my way to Regina – leaving Monday morning."

"Sounds like a nice trip. I love the prairies."

"You travel almost as much as I do, by the sounds of things."

"Yes, I do. I'm just returning from a national tour. It took us into the Northwest Territories and the Yukon. It was amazing. I am coming from booking my last show for this year, which will be held in Fredericton. We did West, North, and then East this year."

The conversation continued as they laughed and joked over breakfast. He was light, funny and had a wit that was endearing. Ruth found herself being caught up in the conversation and began to talk about her dream of driving a truck and travelling the country in a semi. She explained that she had lots of friends who had offered, but those offers never materialized. She did the next best thing. She used truck stops the same as truckers, for food, gas, showers, and necessities. She still hoped she would eventually be able to realize her dream, and set out in a semi for places unknown.

"My name is Dusty Morgan. I am leaving Monday morning; you are more than welcome to join me for the trip if you like."

"Are you serious?" Ruth looked at him wide-eyed.

"Sure am; I wouldn't offer if I wasn't. Take my phone number, think about it, and let me know."

Ruth jotted down his phone number and passed him her business card. "I'm Ruth Higgins. I'll think about it. It was nice chatting with you. Thanks for the company and conversation. Enjoy the rest of your breakfast," she said, gathering her belongings and preparing to leave.

Ruth left the restaurant with visions of her dream about to come true. Did she dare drop everything and go? There was little she had to do she could not do from the road, and she had not had a vacation in a long time. It was August, and the tour was in a lull until fall. As she drove home, her mind continued to spin with the possibilities of taking a trip west with Dusty in the truck.

She pulled into the driveway and unpacked her half-ton from the road trip. She stood in the nook of her dining room and looked at the little Matchbox tractor trailer that had sat there for so many years. The words, "Take the risk or lose the chance," came to mind. She called Ambrose and caught up with him on the phone. She discussed the impromptu conversation she'd had with Dusty over breakfast.

"Why not go? You have wanted to do this all your life. I think it would be good for you. If you trust the guy, then why not?" he said.

Ruth settled down in bed that night and replayed the conversation with Dusty over in her head. He seemed nice and did not appear to be someone to be afraid of. Even if they did not get along, she could always get dropped off somewhere along the route and return home. Ambrose's words continued to play over in her mind, "Why not?"

Ruth awoke to a beautiful Sunday morning. She sat in her rocking chair, sipping her coffee and looking out the window. She was still thinking about the breakfast conversation from the day before. She picked up her cellphone to check her messages, and there was a text from Dusty. Hope you made it home okay. Truck is still leaving Monday.

As she scrolled, she saw the picture he sent of the truck. It was a grey Freightliner. Moose rack, square-nosed, and two chrome stacks on either side just behind the doors. It was perfect. Why not? She thought and dialled his number.

"Hello," came a male voice on the phone that sounded distracted.

"Hello, Dusty? This is Ruth from breakfast yesterday. I hope I'm not interrupting you."

"No, not at all, Ruth. It's good to hear from you."

"If you are serious about letting me come to Regina with you, then I am seriously thinking about taking you up on your offer."

"Absolutely. I would love to have you along. I'm leaving Aulac in the morning. If you can get yourself here, it would be great to have the company. Regina is a long trip. It is always good to have some company along."

"I'm not sure how I'm going to get there, but I'll get there. Call you back shortly," Ruth laughed as she hung up the phone.

Ruth started to pack for the trip. Her mind whirled trying to figure out a way to get to Aulac for the next day. It was a three-hour drive. She did not want to leave her pickup unattended at the Aulac truck stop for such a long time. She had always been adventurous, and this was certainly an adventure that would be right up her alley. Once her backpack was packed, she settled down to try and figure out how she was going to get there.

She called Ambrose to tell him of her plans, and he was quick to suggest, "Why not take the bus? There must be one today you can catch." Ruth checked the bus schedule online and found one leaving at four that afternoon. Ambrose could drive her to the depot, drop her off, and take her half-ton back home. She quickly purchased her ticket online and called Dusty back.

"Hi, Dusty, it's Ruth again. I can come by bus. I will take a cab from the bus depot to Aulac and meet you there tonight, if that works?"

"No cab required. I will pick you up. See you then."

Ruth called Cindy, her best friend. Cindy was excited for her, yet cautious about her travelling with a stranger alone. Cindy knew how much this trip would mean to Ruth. Cindy jotted down contact information, details of the company, and what little information Ruth could provide.

Cindy asked Ruth for details about Dusty. His looks, personality, where he was from. "Who knows what might transpire or come out of this Ruth?" Cindy was a hopeless romantic and was always hoping Ruth would find someone to make her happy. She knew Ruth's ex-husband and what he had put Ruth through over the forty years they were together. Cindy was excited about the possibility of a new man in Ruth's life.

"Don't get carried away, Cindy. It is just a truck trip. I have travelled with the tour for years and have been around many men. Dusty is no different. I am not looking for romance. I am going on vacation. I will be in touch throughout the trip, and I will see you when I get back.

"Be careful, be safe and have fun. I can't wait to hear all about it when you get back."

Ruth called Connie and Dorothy, Bob's daughters, and told them of the opportunity she was about to take. They were excited for her. The sisters had watched her grow up around the big rigs and they knew how much she wanted to be a truck driver. Why, they never knew, but they always cheered her on, hoping for her to one day realize her dream. They wished her well and made her promise to come and visit as soon as she got back.

Ruth called Abby in England. Abby was concerned with her mother's new adventure and full of questions about the driver and her mother's safety. Did she know what she was doing? Abby was always the responsible one, trying to take care of everyone. She had left home for

England with a suitcase, knowing no one and not having a job when she got there.

Abby was much like Ruth, flying by the seat of her pants and travelling to foreign destinations whenever she could. Ruth had been apprehensive about Abby moving to England. But Abby was an adult, and there was nothing she could do. Ruth was in tears the night she waved goodbye to her at the airport security gate, and prayed she would be fine.

Abby was a beautiful young woman. Her dark wavy hair hung almost to her waist. She was tall and slender, with brown eyes and a sparkling smile. She ran to stay fit and had completed more than one half marathon. She was a smart, resourceful young woman and had a good head on her shoulders.

She had done well in England and was working as an office manager with an international finance company. Abby was following her own dream. Ruth promised to stay in touch from the road, told her she loved her, and hung up.

The conversation between herself and Ambrose as they drove to the bus depot was filled with questions and answers about Dusty and her plans. Ambrose wanted all the necessary contact information —who he worked for, his full name, and his telephone number.

Ruth looked at the young man who sat beside her and marvelled at how much he had grown. He was well over six feet tall and was a very fit two hundred and sixty-odd pounds. He had played rugby in high school and had been careful to keep himself physical fit. He had dark hair, dark eyes, and a closely trimmed beard.

Ambrose had always been his mother's biggest fan. He was used to her adventurous ways, and knew being a truck driver was something she had always dreamed of doing. He dropped Ruth and her backpack off at the bus station. They hugged before Ruth boarded the bus. "Have fun, Mom. You deserve this." He turned and waved as Ruth stepped onto the bus and prepared to find her seat.

Ruth looked out the window of the bus and watched the landscape speed by. She could not believe she was dropping everything and heading out with a strange truck driver on what was to be a five-day trip to Regina. She called Spencer, the producer of the tour, and told him she was going to Regina in a semi. She would keep up to date on tour business from the road. They had worked together for a little over six years, and he knew about her love for big rigs. He was concerned for her safety and made her promise to keep in touch.

The excitement started to build in Ruth as the bus continued to roll along. She could not believe in a couple of hours she would be spending her first night with a strange man in a big truck. It was not a situation that was foreign to her. She had travelled with many professional entertainers over the years, and had spent many nights alone in hotel rooms with a variety of different men.

She was a firm believer in men and women being friends without romance or sexual relationships getting in between. There were two bunks in the truck. She had been promised one of them. As far as she was concerned, this trip was no different than the many trips she had spent on the road with musicians. The prospect of living a lifelong dream had overshadowed any doubt in her mind she was doing the right thing.

The bus pulled into the depot in Sackville, New Brunswick, and stopped for the passengers to disembark. She stepped off onto the ground and saw the Freightliner from the text message pull in behind the bus. Her heart skipped a beat as she realized the truck was there to pick her up. She hoisted her backpack over her shoulder and walked slowly towards it. The driver's door swung open. The man she had shared breakfast with the previous day climbed down and stepped out onto the ground.

A big smile came across his face as she walked forward and said, "Hi, there," almost laughing as she said it.

His eyes sparkled as he smiled and walked towards the passenger door to open it for her. "Hi. Did you have a good trip?"

"Yes, thank you." She threw her backpack up onto the seat, gripped the outside grab handle, and pulled herself up into the cab.

Dusty closed the door behind her, walked around, and climbed up into the driver's seat. Ruth was too excited to be able to say much. He asked questions about her decision and explained to her what she could expect. He told her there may be a weight problem with the truck and the machine he was hauling. These things would be decided in the morning. He drove the truck out of the bus depot parking lot and turned onto the feeder ramp for the highway.

The sun was going down, and the sunset was beautiful as they made their way back to the truck stop. He continued to chat, and all she could do was nod or answer with brief, short sentences. Her stomach was filled with butterflies. She was so excited about what she was doing and had pinched herself more than once to see if she was dreaming.

Dusty had been running bobtail to pick her up. When they arrived at the truck stop, he swung the truck in front of the tandem axle jeep and float, and proceeded to back up. The truck jolted as the jaws of the fifth wheel connected with the king pin. Dusty tugged the trailer brake on the dash to make sure the connection was solid before stepping out of the truck to reconnect the glad hands.

Ruth climbed down out of the truck. Once he was finished making sure the truck was reconnected to the load, they walked towards the diner for supper. The waitresses knew him. They were happy to hear the story of the woman who had always dreamed of travelling in a semi, and were tickled Dusty was going to take Ruth to Regina.

Dusty and Ruth ate and chatted. They realized they had quite a bit in common. It seemed they would get along for the five days necessary to make Regina by Friday.

Dusty explained the trip, how long it would take, where the stops would be, and how he was hoping to get away early in the morning after the weigh in. They returned to the truck and Dusty stayed outside while Ruth changed her clothes and got ready to spend her first night in the cab of the Freightliner. She looked around and was amazed at how compact the truck was, and how much stuff could be stored to ensure the comfort of the drivers.

There were two almost-three-quarter-sized bunk beds, a microwave, and a mini fridge. She peaked behind the closet door on the left and saw where Dusty hung his clothes. In the other closet to the right were shelves where Dusty kept his dishes, laundry detergent, dryer sheets, a toaster, and a variety of odds and ends.

There was another small closet under his clothes closet that held his dry goods. There were two drawers under each closet. One held the utensils, the other his paperwork. Cubby holes with netting extended the full perimeter of the inside of the truck above the windshield and side windows. Captured behind the netting were information binders, paper towels, bread, and a road atlas, along with numerous company ball caps he had collected.

There were two seats, and sitting on the floor between them were a pair of sneakers and a pair of work boots that served as extra cup and bottle holders. A garbage bag hung on the arm rest of the passenger seat. Stuck to the inside of the windshield was an E-Z Pass monitor for direct passage through toll booths.

Dusty had removed all the plastic bins from the top bunk and had stacked them, one on top of the other, on the passenger seat. The bins held his rain and safety gear, hard hat, safety vest, and extra clothing. In the morning, when the top bunk wasn't being used by Ruth, they would be returned there for the day while they travelled.

Dusty did not seem to have any problem shifting the bins and his belongings around to make Ruth comfortable. He seemed to be happy she was travelling with him. She could see it on his face. It would be something different from the normal routine he usually experienced on the road.

Ruth felt an instant connection between the two of them. He was a big man, a little over six feet tall, with broad shoulders. His arms were muscular from the heavy lifting that came from the work he did. He had short, brown hair that was graying. He was clean shaven, and his brown eyes sparkled as he talked to her. They revealed a gentleness and kindness about him. She was not afraid of him. He was soft spoken and had a smile that was contagious.

Ruth was surprised at how comfortable she was around him and how an immediate feeling of being in a safe place seemed to engulf her. They had met less than twenty-four hours before, and Ruth had no problem with the idea of spending the night in the cab.

Ruth crawled into her bunk as Dusty adjusted the air conditioning to make sure she was comfortable. He had been concerned about her comfort since she had arrived. Being from Newfoundland, he was a joker and cracked jokes continually. His accent made it hard to understand him at times, but it was not long before she caught on to his unique way of speaking.

Ruth lay down in her bunk and gazed through the skylight of the truck while Dusty busied himself getting settled in the bunk below. He talked about his trucking friends, his trucking adventures, and she told him about life on the road with professional entertainers. He seemed genuinely interested in her, her background, and how she came to work with musicians. She closed her eyes and, with a smile on her face, fell asleep to the sound of his voice.

Morning came early. Dusty's alarm rang, and he was up and gone. Ruth was used to being able to get up and leisurely start her day with a cup of coffee. It normally took her an hour or more to really wake up. She was used to late nights of performances, and even later mornings. Being up at the crack of dawn was certainly out of the ordinary.

She climbed out of the bunk and grabbed her backpack to head inside to get changed and ready for the day. There were showers available, and she helped herself to one. The hot water cascaded over her, and she quickly washed, got out, and dried herself off. There was no time to waste. They were on a schedule and she did not want to hold Dusty up.

While she toweled her hair dry, Ruth caught a glimpse of herself in the mirror. She was a very young looking fifty-eight years old. She had often been mistaken for being in her late forties. She dyed her hair its natural brown and wore it cropped close to her head. She never wanted to take the time necessary to style it. All Ruth had to do was run her fingers through it. Her eyes were brown and had a life in them that revealed she was up for any kind of fun. Her smile was crooked because of a childhood horseback riding injury. She called it her pirate smiled. She liked it.

Ruth pulled on a fresh pair of blue jeans and pulled a T-shirt over her head. It was primarily all she ever wore. She leaned over and tugged at her cowboy boots as her feet slipped into them. Even at the age of fifty-eight, she was a true tomboy.

She examined herself again in the mirror. She never wore makeup, and her medium build was fit. Her weight was well distributed within her five-foot-five-inch frame. She was still getting used to the glasses she had to wear, but was adjusting to them and decided she liked them. She was ready to go.

Dusty was waiting for Ruth in the restaurant. "I took the liberty of ordering for you. I hope you don't mind, but we are a wee bit pressed for time."

"Not at all. What am I having?"

"Regular breakfast fare: eggs, bacon, hash browns, toast, and, of course, breakfast wouldn't be complete without coffee. Lots and lots of coffee."

Dusty chatted with everyone as they passed by. He was open and friendly. Breakfast with him was so different from those Ruth had shared with some of the musicians. She enjoyed eating with him. With their plates empty, they were ready to go and headed out to the truck. Dusty talked about the pre-trip inspection and showed her where the information was recorded on the Electronic Logging Device, also known as an E-Log or ELD.

Dusty explained that a pre-trip inspection was a complete inspection of the mechanics of the truck and trailer. This was mandatory every morning to ensure the truck and trailer were safe for the road. Drivers checked lights, engine, air bags, brakes—going over every detail. All the information was recorded on the ELD and could be seen by those working in the company office.

The truck was satellite-tracked; thus, the company knew at all times the location of the truck and what was happening. The ELD also kept track of the drivers. Where they were, what they were doing, the hours they were driving, and each time the truck stopped and the reason why.

"Since you are travelling along, you may as well know how things work." He explained what all the switches were on the dashboard. He turned the key to start the engine, pushed in the air brakes, moved the gear shift into position, and the truck slowly moved forward to the scale.

"We have to weigh in before we leave. That way I know how heavy the load is. I will pull onto the scale. If you could get out and let me know when the back tires of the float are over the line, I would appreciate it."

Ruth opened the door and climbed down to the ground. It was a long way down for her. She had to practice the three-point contact rule, one hand on the grab handled, one on the door, and one foot on the step to ensure she did not slip and fall getting in or out of the truck.

Dusty moved the truck, jeep, and float slowly forward. She motioned to him when he was fully on the scale, and waited. When the weigh was done, she climbed back up into the truck. "We will have to move the excavator about six inches backwards to distribute the weight a little better and weigh it again."

He pulled the truck forward and back into the parking lot. He got out and started to unchain the 350 John Deere Excavator sitting on the float. Ruth watched in amazement as he went about his work. He was precise and efficient in releasing the chains and binders. He moved quickly, with grace and ease for a man of his stature.

He had to stretch to open the door of the excavator, even though he was a little over six feet tall. He pried the door open, pulled himself in, and started the machine. Systematically he moved the joy sticks of the excavator and started to inch it backwards, until he guessed he had moved it the required six inches to accommodate the necessary requirement for weight distribution on the scale.

Dusty climbed down, closed the door and proceeded to replace the chains and binders to secure it to the float. "That should do it." Dusty pulled himself up into the cab of the truck and Ruth started to walk across the parking lot towards the scale. He had to make a wide swing to position himself properly on the scale. Ruth stood waiting to motion to him when the back tires were over the line for the second time.

"Looks good; come on in." Ruth heard a female voice come over the scale loudspeaker.

Dusty moved the truck off the scale and parked. He walked into the building to pick up the weigh slip. Ruth was starting to realize there was a lot more involved in trucking than just sitting behind the wheel, driving, and waiting for the lights to change. Dusty returned with a yellow slip of paper in his hand and looked at Ruth. "Okay, we are ready to go. Hop in."

Ruth opened the door and climbed back up to the passenger seat. Dusty turned on the radio, pushed in the air brakes, and dropped the truck into gear. They started forward and rolled out of the truck stop parking lot. Ruth could not believe her dream trip was about to begin.

CHAPTER 2
Regina,
Two Hours at a Time

The sun was shining and the truck moved along at a good clip. Dusty explained that the trucks were governed. "We can only travel so fast. The trucks won't go any faster. This one is governed at about one hundred and ten kilometers an hour. I have been driving her for about three years. She can really pull her weight. My truck number is 309." He looked at her and winked.

"As in 'Phantom 309'? It is one of my favourite trucking songs. Why don't you put the name on the truck?"

"I would if R.A.E. would let me. But for now, she's just 309."

Dusty and Ruth laughed, joked, and talked about their lives to pass the time. Dusty chatted on the CB Radio and his cellphone Bluetooth in between. The truckers all kept in touch with each other—like a check-in system to make sure everyone was okay and where they all were. Ruth was impressed by the way they genuinely cared about each other. They were a group unlike any she had encountered before.

They were later than expected leaving Aulac, having been delayed by the weigh in. It was almost five o'clock when they were finally approaching Fredericton. The day had passed quickly. Ruth had been listening closely to Dusty stories and gazing out the window at the landscape.

Things looked so different from her seat in the truck in comparison to when she was travelling in her half ton. It seemed like she was driving through the clouds. When they crossed over the Jemseg Bridge, she looked down into the river. There did not seem to be much room between them and the concrete barrier that protected traffic from going over the edge and into the water below.

As they approached the New Maryland exit, Ruth started to sniff the air. "Do you smell something? It smells like oil burning."

Dusty checked the gauges just as the lights started to blink on the dashboard. "Damn, something's wrong," and Ruth could feel the truck starting to slow down.

He pulled over and got out to check and see what was going on. The smell of diesel fuel and engine oil were strong. Ruth stayed in the truck. She did not want to interfere with his work. He was visibly upset. She did not want to frustrate him with questions.

Dusty climbed back in the cab and grabbed his cellphone. He called dispatch to explain the situation and the mechanical problems they were experiencing. "I'm not sure what's wrong. She just got out of the shop a few days ago. She should have been good to go. Let me know what you want me to do."

"We are going to be sitting here while dispatch figures out what they are going to do. In the meantime, make yourself comfortable. I'm sorry about this; it is not a very good way to start the trip."

Ruth picked up her phone and started checking her email. "May as well get some work done."

She tried to focus on the emails in front of her on the cellphone screen. She could not help but think her dream trip might come to a sudden halt. She tried to stay positive. If this was all the trip was going to be, then so be it.

Dusty's phone rang, and he listened to the instructions from dispatch on what was going to happen. He hung up and turned to Ruth. "They are sending a tow truck from Truro with another truck. We will switch out when they get here. It could be a long wait. If necessary, the woods are right there for you to use if you need to go."

Ruth finished up her work. "I may as well take a nap. It is about a five-hour drive from Truro. It is going to be late by the time the tow truck gets here," she said standing up and climbing out of the passenger seat.

She reached up to start pulling the plastic bins down from the top bunk. "You can use mine. I'm not going to be needing it. It saves moving all that stuff around." Ruth nodded and crawled into the lower bunk and stretched out. She turned on her Spotify and lay back to relax.

Dusty passed the time talking on the phone to some of his trucker friends, his mother, and a few members of his family. His continuous keeping in touch with everyone was so different than Ruth. She hardly ever called anyone, other than her children and sister, while she was on the road. She posted regularly on social media where she was and pictures of things she had seen throughout the day. People followed her there. She rarely spoke to anyone on the telephone.

Dusty got up from the driver's seat and opened the fridge. "You want a bottle of water?" he said, handing her one from the fridge. Ruth took the water and sat up. Dusty sat on the edge of the bunk to talk while they waited. Time ticked by. They covered an array of different topics. He was an intelligent man with a unique outlook on life. One that Ruth shared.

Ruth finished her water and stretched out, shifting further towards the back of the bunk to give Dusty more room. Space was limited in the truck and one had to make do with the close quarters they were in. It was hard not to feel the other's closeness. Ruth could feel her heart beginning to beat a little faster as she took in the smell of Dusty's body. It was musky and all man. The aroma intoxicated her. She kept shifting herself in the bunk to try and break the spell that was starting to overtake her.

It had been over a year since she had been involved with a man in any way. She could feel the familiar stirrings of physical attraction beginning to grow. She tried to rationalize what was happening. She was there in the dark, in a semi, with a man she barely knew. She tried to think it was just her getting all wrapped up in the moment. She hoisted herself up on one elbow to carry on the conversation they were having without her feelings getting involved.

Dusty turned and looked down at her. He moved forward and lightly kissed her on the lips. Ruth did not move. She looked at him without saying a word. "Well, that went okay. I will try that again," and he moved in to kiss her again, letting it linger longer than the first.

He pulled back and looked her in the eyes as she lay silent, "Are you okay?"

"Yes," Ruth whispered.

Dusty turned and stretched out beside her. He took her in his arms, pulled her close, and kissed her again. Before they knew it, they were kissing passionately, forgetting where they were. His hands travelled her body and moved below her shirt to caress her bare back. She could feel his breath quicken against her skin. His hands continued to move slowly along the curve of her hip and under her T-shirt.

He stood up and removed his tank top. Ruth could feel her loins beginning to stir as they continued to enjoy the newness of each other.

"Are you sure you're okay? I don't want to do anything you are uncomfortable with."

"I'm fine. I'm quite enjoying myself. However, don't you think it might be better to put this off until after the tow truck has come and gone. We can continue what we are doing now, but to take it any further, only to be interrupted by the tow truck, would not be a good thing," she said with a chuckle in her voice.

"You are quite right," Dusty laughed and stretched out beside her. He continued to gently run his hands over her skin. Ruth was surprised at how her body reacted to him. She moved in closer and could feel his manhood growing with passion. She slid her tongue inside his mouth and her breath came in quick short gasps as he massaged her back. She could feel, with each lingering movement, her body react and relax more and more to his touch.

As things began to heat up, the lights of the tow truck driving up in front of them shone through the windshield. "See what I told you," Ruth laughed. Dusty laughed and quickly got up, dressed, and stepped across in front of the driver's seat. He was out the door and gone before Ruth could say any more. She had never seen a man of his size move so fast. She quickly got up and looked out through the windshield. Dusty was talking to the tow truck driver. Ruth could see them preparing to unhook the replacement truck. She started to gather her things and prepare to make the switch.

By the time everything needed was packed up and moved, it was close to midnight. The tow truck driver hooked on to 309 and was on his way. Dusty backed up and you could feel 301 jolt, as she locked into position on the jeep. Dusty shifted gears and they were on the road.

"We are going to have to take a chance," Dusty said with a sly grin on his face. We don't have far to the yard. We're not supposed to be on the highway after dark with a load this size. Under the circumstances, we have no choice, owing to the breakdown. We can't stay parked on the side of the highway all night."

Ruth looked at Dusty as he drove through the darkness. She could still feel his hands on her body and his kiss on her lips. Her body had responded to his touch so quickly. She found herself sitting in the passenger seat longing for his touch. She could not wait to get parked in the yard and resume the events that had taken place a few hours earlier.

They made the turn into the yard, and Dusty put the truck in park and pulled the air brakes. He unhooked the curtain from behind his seat and slid it across in front of the windshield to block out the lights of the yard, and to ensure their privacy for sleeping. Ruth did the same with the curtain on her side and attached the Velcro strip in the center.

Dusty slipped out of the driver's seat and stood up. He took Ruth's hand, helping her stand up out of the passenger seat. She stood still in front of him, looking into his eyes. He took her in his arms, pulled her close, and kissed her. "Are you sure you're okay with this?"

"Yes, I am sure," Ruth whispered as she wrapped her arms around his neck to kiss him again.

He slowly took the hem of her T-shirt in his hands and pulled it over her head. He never took his eyes off her. She stood in front of him as he reached behind her, undid the clasp of her bra, and let it fall to the floor. Ruth found herself feeling shy, like on a first date. It had been a long time since a man had looked at and touched her this way. She felt a rush of heat run through her body as she reached down and pulled off his tank top. He pulled her close and kissed her again. Harder this time. His passion began to rise, and his longing for her increased.

He turned her towards the bunk and laid her down before lying down beside her. His hands explored her torso and moved to unbuckle her belt. He smoothly opened the button and zipper to her jeans. She could not move; she was mesmerized by what was happening. The intensity of their coupling began to grow. He slipped off her jeans and dropped them to the floor. He stood up, unbuckled his own belt, and let his pants ease down over his hips.

Dusty's body was solid. His muscles were obvious. He had the features of what could only be described as a real man, one that worked hard. He stepped out of his pants. Ruth repositioned herself on the bunk, allowing him more room beside her when he laid back down. The smoothness of his skin was like silk as she ran her hands down his back and over his bare buttocks.

Ruth's breathing quickened as he pulled back from kissing her, "Are you sure you are okay?"

"Yes, I am sure. Now, stop asking," and she pulled him to her to kiss him again.

Dusty moved his mouth down over her nipples and over her stomach resting at the top of her mound. He licked and kissed her as she spread her legs to welcome his tongue. Her back arched as his hot tongue began to explore and probe her vagina, making her moan with pleasure.

He took her legs and placed them over his shoulders to open her up. Pleasure overtook her and she shuddered as he continued to lick and probe her inner core. She drew him up to her mouth and kissed him hard. When he entered her for the first time a small, muffled, deep-throated scream escaped her lips.

Dusty lifted her to him and, placing both hands on her buttocks, began to rock her slowly. Ruth joined the rhythm and soon felt herself beginning to let go again. Dusty could not hold back his passion for her any longer.

They climaxed together and Ruth felt him go limp. She held him close, looking into his smiling eyes as he rolled over and lay down beside her, exhausted.

Ruth was the first one to speak. "That was amazing. It has been over a year for me and that was certainly worth waiting for."

"That was incredible," he mumbled, with a chuckle in his voice.

They lay in each other's arms, engrossed in their own thoughts. Ruth curled up next to him resting her head on his shoulder and yawned, "I think, I'm ready to go to sleep. It has been a long day with a perfect end."

"We will have an early start in the morning," Dusty said, kissing her on the top of the head.

They woke up to the sound of Dusty's alarm. Ruth was uncertain if it would be awkward, as they had met less than forty-eight hours before. Dusty seemed so easygoing. Ruth felt she had known him for years. Dusty pointed out a diner across the street, and they walked hand in hand towards it for breakfast.

Sometime during the night, Dusty realized the air conditioning in 301 was not working and had already talked to dispatch about stopping to get it fixed. The temperatures in Quebec and Ontario were running at record highs. He would not drive a truck without air conditioning. Dispatch directed him to a garage in Hartland, New Brunswick. They did not know how long it would be in the shop, but the stop was about two hours' drive away. Following breakfast, they were back in the truck, back on the road, and heading to Hartland.

Ruth laughed to herself as they made their way west on the Trans-Canada Highway. The truck trip had started on Monday afternoon and the delivery was supposed to be made in Regina on Friday. They were already running behind schedule, because of the breakdown. Now, they were stopping again for the air conditioning. Twenty-four hours later, and they had only made it about four hours' drive up the road.

Dusty pulled into the garage parking lot and disappeared into the shop. Ruth swung open the door, took hold of the grab handle, and hopped down onto the ground. She had started to ignore the three-point contact rule and had nicknamed the handle the Batman pole as she swung herself out of the truck and to the ground.

While Dusty was inside making arrangements for the air conditioning repairs, Ruth started to wander around the parking lot looking at all the new trucks lined up for sale. They were Western Stars. Some of them were large enough to be considered tiny houses on wheels. She longingly looked at them, dreaming of a day when she might be able to drive one, or own one, of her own.

It took a good portion of the afternoon to get the air conditioning up and running properly. Once the bill was settled through R.A.E., they were on their way. They would not get too far tonight, as daylight was already becoming a precious commodity. They were driving against the clock. They pulled off the highway at the Grey Rock Truck Stop exit.

Dusty prepared to maneuver the one hundred and five feet around the turn. It was a tight turn for Dusty and proved to put his twenty-seven years of driving skills to the test. "Can you look and see if I am going to hit the light standard as I make this turn?"

Ruth rolled down the window, leaned out, and looked back, "You're not going to make it."

"Damn!"

He stopped and put the truck in reverse to back up and give the truck a wider berth to make the swing." What about now?"

"Yeah, there's room now, but there will only be inches to spare."

Dusty moved slowly forward. They could feel the float tire hit and roll over the curb as they made the swing to take the road leading to the truck stop, which was part of the Grey Rock Power Centre, near Edmundston, New Brunswick. Dusty got out and began to refuel. When he had the nozzles properly placed in the fuel tanks, he walked around the float, checking on the lights and making sure everything was working the way it should be. After a close inspection, he noticed a couple of lights on the back of the float were not functioning. He tapped at them. They did not light up.

"Looks like we won't get too far again tonight. I can't travel with lights out. We will have to find a place to get them fixed before we go any further." Dusty took his cell-phone from the clip on his hip and dialled dispatch.

"At this rate, I'm going to call this trip, 'Regina—two hours at a time.' We have been on the road two days and we have not even left New Brunswick," she laughed.

"Welcome to the trucking business," replied Dusty as he took the fuel nozzle from the tank and hooked it back in place.

His cellphone rang, and when he hung up, he yelled, "Jump in, there's a place not far from here. If it is a simple fix, and they can fix her up for us, we can get moving."

Ruth opened the door and climbed in, "Here we go again."

They arrived at the garage and waited for a mechanic to show up. It was after hours, and someone had to be called in to take a look at the float. Ruth was learning that people who were connected to the smooth running of trucks worked around the clock.

Dispatchers and mechanics in most cases were available twenty-four hours a day to meet the needs of truckers. There was always someone a trucker could call for help—tire companies, roadside mechanics. Anyone and everyone were available to keep the trucks rolling towards their destinations with as little delay as possible.

Ruth wandered around the yard as the men worked together to try and figure out where the lights were shorting out. Daylight was fading and it looked like another night in New Brunswick. The men worked until daylight was gone. "They won't be able to finish it up tonight. Looks like it is a little more complicated than a quick fix. We are going to drop the jeep and float and leave it here. We can bobtail back to the truck stop. We will stay there tonight. They have showers, a Tim Hortons, and pretty good food. The mechanics will be in first thing in the morning." Ruth nodded in agreement and climbed back up into the cab.

This truck stop Ruth had never visited before tonight. She knew most of them, since she travelled back and forth across the country on a regular basis. It was a newer one, and the showers were large and clean. She enjoyed the heat of the water as it ran over her body. She was surprised by the lack of aches and pains she felt from the long duration of sitting in the passenger seat without a break. She had not thought of the breakdowns truckers might experience. Not only was she getting a dream trip, she was actually living the life of a trucker and seeing, first-hand, the numerous troubles they could encounter.

Dusty was tired, even though there had been very little driving over the past two days. The stress of the breakdowns easily showed on his face. Ruth was surprised he was still able to maintain his positive attitude and quirky sense of humour. Ruth was not sure whether it was because she was along for the ride, or if this was the way he was all the time.

There had been tense moments on the phone as he explained the trouble to his dispatcher. He tried to defend himself about being behind schedule. "There is nothing I can do about it. The truck and float breaking down is not my fault and was not in the plans. I will get there when I get there, once she is fixed and running right. I will make up the time," he barked into the phone as he hung up.

Ruth order the lobster roll, and they sat and discussed the day's events. Ruth had so many questions, and Dusty seemed eager to answer them. So far, they had not travelled very far, but they were still moving ahead. Ruth was happy they had not had to turn around and go back. She could continue to work on the tour from the road. It did not matter how far she travelled, as long as she could stay along for the ride.

Following the meal, Ruth and Dusty returned to the truck to settle down for the night. They had discussed their lovemaking from the night before and decided one bunk was big enough for the two of them. Ruth was surprised at how easily she had been ignited by his touch and how much she was enjoying their time together. Dusty seemed to feel the same. He had expressed more than once how amazing he felt their lovemaking had been and seemed eager to continue where they left off the night before.

As they snuggled together in the bunk, his hands began to explore her body. His touch sparked an instant flame inside her. She moaned as he spread the lips of her pussy with his fingers, searching for the hood of her clit. She leaned into him and began to kiss him, nibbling on his lower lip.

Her hands wandered over his chest and stomach to find his manhood. She took his cock in her hand and began to slowly stroke him. They hugged each other closely. They both were learning the special places that would set fire to their souls.

"What do you want? Tell me what you want?" Dusty said in a deep husky voice, breaking the silence.

"Why tell you what I want? Isn't the idea of new love and lovemaking finding out by exploring what the other wants and likes?" Ruth replied nipping at his lower lip.

Dusty lifted himself up on his elbow and looked lovingly into her eyes. He kissed her lightly and then placed his hand behind her head, becoming more forceful and passionate. Ruth was dizzy with his ardour and seemed to lose all concept of time. Her head spun with the feelings of sensuality building between them.

He swung her around on top of him to straddle his hips. She could feel him deep inside her. She began to rock rhythmically and took his hands to steady herself. Their excitement began to build, and together they soared, elevating each other to new climactic heights of pleasure.

As they lay side by side in the bunk, spent, Ruth murmured, "How you are able to make my body respond to you is such unfamiliar territory for me. I have never felt this weak before."

"I know exactly what you mean," Dusty moved his arm around her neck and drew her close to him so Ruth could curl up next to him as they fell asleep.

They were up early. After picking up coffee and oatmeal, they made their way back to the garage. The mechanics were already working on the float. Dusty was hopeful they would be on the road soon. Ruth busied herself concentrating on tour business. She had been in touch with Spencer and things were coming together smoothly for the fall schedule. Ruth began to wonder, as she worked, if she actually wanted to continue with the tour in the fall. She loved being on the road with Dusty, even under the circumstances of breakdowns. She began to think, trucking may be where her heart was beginning to call her.

The float lights were finally fixed and they were pulling out onto the Trans-Canada Highway, heading west. It would be a long day. The sun was shining and the sky was clear. The weather man was calling for a perfect late summer day. There would be no heavy rain or winds to contend with or slow them down. It would be a good day to begin the process of making up lost time.

Ruth sat contentedly in the passenger seat watching the landscape roll by. Things looked so different from her perch in the truck. Dusty turned the radio on, found the best country music station, and began to sing. He had a fabulous voice and Ruth joined him in the songs she knew. They sang, laughed, and talked about their lives beyond the cab.

Dusty had a bad experience with marriage, the same as herself, although hers had lasted far longer than his. He told her of returning home after having been married for about five years, and finding his wife in bed with another man. The woman had tried to encourage him to give up trucking. He would not do it. He loved his job. He had worked hard to get himself to the level of being able to transport oversized and heavy haul loads. His ex-wife did not understand his passion for trucking or being on the road. He had been driving for twenty-seven years. He was not about to stop, until the time when he could drive no longer. Trucking was in his blood. He thought he could never find a woman who understood his passion for being behind the wheel.

Ruth understood. She had the same longings and loved being on the road, behind the wheel of her Chevy. She felt a sense of freedom and would live on the road full time if she could. With the tour, she had been able to do that. She could have flown around, getting to places faster and with far less worry and hassle, but she loved the open road ahead of her.

She had learned to live as a minimalist and travel light. She camped and slept in the back of her half ton. She had a piece of foam, a sleeping bag, and a pillow laid out on the floor of the backseat for when she needed to stop for the night. She already lived like a trucker, just in a different way. She liked being able to stop whenever she wanted to explore. She had taken many different side roads to see where they would lead.

Ruth loved to camp and enjoyed travelling in the spring, summer, and fall. The winter months were tricky, because of the snow and ice. On the sunny days, when the roads were bare, Ruth enjoyed driving through the snow-covered countryside. She had travelled across the country in every season. Ruth was always able to appreciate the changes she saw along the way.

When the weather was warm, Ruth would pull into truck stops, campgrounds, and roadside turnouts. She would set up a campfire and enjoy the nature that surrounded her. She did not mind travelling alone and was becoming accustom to it.

There were times when she had to transport musicians, and it annoyed her to have someone else in the vehicle. Their endless chatter. The necessity of changing the radio station to suit their tastes. Having to stop to accommodate their personal needs. They wanted to get from point A to point B without truly enjoying the scenery around them. They did not appreciate the landscape, the scenic outlooks, the natural beauty they were seeing.

Ruth liked the freedom of not having to travel with passengers. It seemed the only person she could travel with comfortably was Spencer, the producer of the tour. They had developed a great travelling relationship over the six years they had been working together. They understood each other and shared the same interests of stopping on the road and enjoying the journey.

The new experience of trucking had started Ruth thinking it might be time to make a career change. She started to think it might be time to start living her dream. Spencer was living his dream through her, by travelling across the country and performing. He was not only the producer of the show, but also handled the lights, sound, and technical aspects of the show. They worked closely together and had developed the tour over time, which fulfilled both their desires.

Ruth wanted to travel, and with the development of the tour, she was able to do so. Otherwise, she would not be able to afford to do all the things she wanted to do. Through the tour, she was seeing so many new things, places and meeting such wonderful people. The more she was on the road, the more she wanted to be.

As she sat next to Dusty in the Freightliner rolling down the road towards Regina, she began to visualize herself behind the wheel. Why not? Why not look into it? she thought. At least on this trip she would learn what trucking was all about. Ruth decided to listen, watch, learn, and help out where she could. This would be more than a living-the-dream kind of trip. This could be a learning experience for a future career.

Dusty and Ruth made good time and were finally out of New Brunswick. It was Wednesday, and it was impossible for them to make Regina by Friday. Dusty was determined to make up as much time as possible. There would be little stopping, and long hours of sitting in the passenger seat awaited her. Ruth knew what annoyed her when she travelled with passengers. She was determined to enjoy the ride and conversation without interrupting the schedule needed to make up the lost time.

Dusty was a remarkable man. He described where he was from in Newfoundland and the small-town environment in which he grew up. He was dedicated to his family. He called his mother faithfully every morning and every evening to let her know what his driving plans were for the day. He felt responsible for her since the passing of his father a little over a year before. He told Ruth about his brother, who also lived at home.

When Dusty was home, he enjoyed a solitude away from people at a cabin in the woods. There he could wake up to a full glass window that looked out onto the forest. He detailed the occasional moose that walked by, and other animals that would venture into his view. What he described sounded like heaven to Ruth. How she longed for a place to be able to escape from the stresses of the world. She wanted to wake up, be able to sit outside, have her coffee in the morning with only the sounds of nature around her.

Ruth sat studying him as he drove. There was a relaxation about him when he was behind the wheel. He chatted with the other truckers as they exchanged information, jokes, and general conversation about work. The comradery among them was endearing. They were all in the same boat. Out on the road alone, driving to their various destinations, to make their pickups and deliveries. Some called to talk and kill time. Others called for council with their personal lives and how to approach work-related issues.

There were Byron, George, Thomas, Walt, Vernon, Nathen, and others. Some were married, some divorced, and others struggling to make ends meet. Truckers were no different than anyone else. Dusty was the comedian among the group. He kept everyone in stitches with one-liners and jokes. They were quite a bunch, and Ruth was quickly becoming attached to them all.

Dusty described the women who worked for the company, and how some had come and gone. There was one who travelled with her dog and was involved with one of the other truckers in the company fleet. There was a man-and-wife team who drove together. There had been another woman driver, but she had broken her ankle and was no longer able to drive. She was recovering at home. They all stayed in touch with her to make sure everything was running smoothly.

The way the truckers looked after one another showed their compassion and empathy. They all realized it could easily be one of them. Dusty had had one serious accident in the United States that landed him in the hospital for a few days before he was able to be transported home to recuperate. Byron had been off the road and totalled his truck when he went into a skid on black ice. They all realized, climbing in their cabs every day, it could be their last day on the road. So, they kept in touch, encouraged each other, and offered up general support for whatever each of them needed.

They all kept in close touch with their loved ones at home. Wives and girlfriends were struggling with young children and the activities of everyday life. Vehicle breakdowns and household mishaps were common among their conversations. The women behind the wheel would keep up on children and how their school work was coming along. The truckers let them know, even though they may be miles from home, they were still interested in their everyday lives.

It was a little more difficult for the female truckers in the industry. Dusty and Ruth discussed the percentage of female to male drivers. It averaged to about three percent. Ruth agreed. While she had been on the road with Dusty, they encountered very few women behind the wheel.

It was a hard job being away from home. For women who wanted a home and family, long-haul trucking certainly was not a smart career choice. A day job of driving a truck around a city would work for a woman, if they wanted children. The cab of a truck was not a great place to bring up a child. There certainly was room, but it would not be fun for a baby or a toddler to spend ten to twelve hours of their day strapped in a car seat.

Ruth had been reading about women in the industry in the magazines she saw in the trucker lounges. There were all kinds of incentive programs to try and entice more women to become drivers. It had been statically proven: women had fewer accidents, and that helped the company with their insurance premium bottom line.

There were many groups and organizations made up of women for women. They were dedicated to recruiting female drivers. It was a hard life for a woman. There were men who resented women in the industry, and they were not long in letting the women know how they felt. Women took a lot of negative comments and were not respected by some of their male colleagues.

The wives of the male drivers were not happy either when women were doing their training and having to ride along in the trucks with their husbands. It was a feeling that was everywhere when women entered a male-dominated industry. There were always those wives who thought they were going to lose their husbands to a woman with whom they were working so closely.

Voice recorders were installed in truck cabs to protect the male drivers from any kind of backlash from training a female driver. Most male drivers refused to train a woman under any circumstances, and there were few female trainers in the industry. For women, it was a hard industry to get into and feel comfortable.

These men and women were on the road anywhere from three to four weeks at a time, in all kinds of weather. Dusty told her there were times he did not get home for six to eight weeks. His job was a specialty, and there were only two others in the company that hauled oversized and heavy haul.

He had worked for nineteen years hauling vans and refrigeration units and was happy when he was given the opportunity with R.A.E. to tackle the oversized and heavy-haul loads. The loads paid better, and there were few who had mastered the art in that part of the industry. Dusty was respected for his ability to get the job done and make the deliveries on time.

41

The sun started to set as they crossed the provincial borderline into Ontario. It had been a long day on the road for both of them. They had stopped only to refuel at a truck stop off Highway 30, the ring road around Montreal. There was a small diner there that Dusty knew, which served delicious poutine. The poutine was delectable, and Ruth added a smoke meat sandwich to go with it. She did not know about the diner. She normally stopped at a spot off Highway 20. This was a welcome alternative, as her spot would not accommodate a tractor trailer.

They pulled into the truck stop at Napanee and into the fuelling line. Dusty got out to refuel and Ruth headed in to use the washroom. This seemed to be her biggest challenge during the trip. Her bladder had to learn that stopping quickly to go was not an option in this industry. When Dusty travelled alone, he did as all the other male drivers, normally using an empty milk carton, water bottle, or some kind of container without ever having to leave the truck. For female drivers, it was a bit more challenging. Ruth thought to herself, a wide-mouth container, a portable camping unit, or some form of female urination device would have to be an obvious choice for a female driver.

The day had been beautiful for the drive. The weather was hot and humid when they exited the truck in Ontario. They put their names on the shower list and went in to relax in the trucker lounge, waiting for their shower numbers to be called. Refuelling with over three hundred litres of diesel fuel allowed each of them a free shower. Ruth was used to paying over eleven dollars to take a shower, as her Chevy could not hold the required litres of gas to garner a free one.

Dusty was treating her like an employee of the company and she was learning how to input information and operate the ELD. In the mornings, during the pre-trip inspections, Dusty would go over all the working parts of the truck and float. He would point out the important things to look for when doing the inspection. The tires, glad hands, electrical connections, brakes, fluids, lights, anything and everything that made the truck and float safer on the highway. He was always checking the chains and binders to make sure they were tight and had not come loose while they were driving.

Dusty was conscious of everything it seemed. There was so much to check and Ruth wondered as she followed him through the inspections whether she had the mechanical mind necessary to learn each and every part name. She was able to keep track and know the system of her pick up, but to know the basics of the tractor, jeep, and float was another thing.

Dusty told her about having to remove the beacon lights to be within the Ontario Highway rules and guidelines of travelling with an oversized and heavy haul load. He had to replace them with signage and red flags to alert drivers to the size of the load. It would be a big fine if they were stopped by Ministry of Transportation officials.

Their weight was always being checked as they pulled into the scale houses sitting on the side of the road. Sometimes they were instructed to pass by, but most times, the indicator sign would request they pull in. They had to drive across the weigh scale to ensure they were within the proper weight ranges for the loads they were carrying. Sometimes they were instructed to come inside to show written proof they had all the proper permits to be travelling through the province.

Some trucks were pulled over and individually inspected to make sure they were mechanically sound. This could include a very detailed inspection. The Ministry of Transportation officers were very meticulous and looked for any little thing that may be out of place. They inspected the logbooks to ensure the driver was driving within the required number of hours. Officers were responsible for making sure there was no loose gravel or dirt on the machines and floats that could fly back and strike a passenger car's windshield.

The Freightliner, tandem axle jeep and float, were one hundred and five feet long, almost twelve feet wide, and with the excavator onboard weighed in at a little over one hundred and forty thousand pounds. Dusty explained, 301 was not considered a heavy spec truck designed for larger loads. It moaned on the steeper hills. Dusty continually commented that his usual truck 309 was a heavy spec truck and would have no problem pulling the load they were hauling.

The truck he was driving, 301, was also an automatic, while 309 was an eighteen-speed standard shift. Dusty was not fond of the automatics and liked the control he had over the speed of the truck with the eighteen gears. He did not think the automatics were designed for oversized and heavy haul in the same way the standard trucks were. As he talked, it was more than obvious Dusty missed driving 309 and had become very attached and familiar with the way the truck operated. 301 was taking him time to get adjusted to. He was unfamiliar with the way it handled and had to pay attention a little more closely to keep on top of the mechanics and operation.

Dusty was disappointed that after 309 had spent two weeks getting reserviced, she was back in the garage. He learned from dispatch that 309 had dropped a piston. It would be as long as two weeks before she would be ready for him to drive. He was hoping she would be ready by the time he got back. Dusty talked about a new truck he was waiting to be delivered. 309 had a lot of miles on her and the warranty had run out. A new truck would be essential to keeping him on the road.

Ruth and Dusty spent their nights making love and falling asleep in each other's arms. The trip was turning into more than a dream truck trip across the country. Ruth was always surprised at how easily they had connected on all levels. Their conversations were varied, covering trucking, religion, political happenings with the country, music of all kinds, old television shows, and matters of the heart. This man who seemed to drop into her life from nowhere was becoming a strong influence on Ruth. She was not one to believe in destiny, but she could not help but wonder if their meeting was fated.

Dusty was ten years younger than Ruth. She had always had a personal rule of not becoming involved with men who were more than two years her junior. It was something Ruth had never been comfortable with. She did not know why, but as soon as she found out a potential male partner was more than two years her junior, it was an automatic turn off for her. With Dusty, she did not feel this way. Their relationship from the beginning was comfortable and relaxed, like they had known each other for years.

Now that all the mechanical issues with both truck and float had been resolved, Dusty and Ruth rolled along through the countryside of Ontario. Dusty made the turn in North Bay to take Highway 11, the northern route through Ontario. He hoped to get to Kapuskasing that night, and stops along the way were going to be few and far between. Ruth had never been through Highway 11, and Dusty talked about and pointed out different landmarks.

Ruth usually drove on Highway 17, which ran along the shoreline of Lake Superior, for the scenery. She was interested to see this new highway and always welcomed the chance to take an unfamiliar route. Dusty explained the northern route was used primarily by truckers to avoid the tourist traffic and there were not as many hills making it possible to make better time.

The CB continued to crackle as Dusty connected with passing trucks. He had just hung up the phone from Byron, one of his closest trucking buddies. Byron was not far behind him and they were hoping to meet up in Kapuskasing for the night. Ruth was anxious to meet Byron. She had listened to their conversations, and he sounded like a very interesting character. She was beginning to realize most of the truckers Dusty kept in touch with had their own quirks and unique personalities.

As the highway turned into wilderness, with only woodland to see for a couple of hours, Ruth retreated to the bunk to take a nap. She put her earbuds in and lulled herself in and out of sleep listening to some of her favourite tunes. By the time she had been with Dusty for twenty-four hours, she was no longer concerned about her safety or being able to complete the trip with him.

There was a relationship developing between them, and memories were being made that she would never forget. The more time she spent with him, the more time she wanted to spend with him. There was an intense energy to their lovemaking that was undeniable. Ruth was beginning to think this kind of feeling only came once in a lifetime. She wanted to explore the possibilities of this relationship, hoping it may blossom into something long term for her.

She had her own relationship baggage. She had been cheated on many times and was leery to some degree of entering into another long-term relationship with any man. Dusty's history with women seemed to coincide with her history with men. She had met quite a few men over the years and had dated a lot, but her trust issues were some of her biggest obstacles. She had been married for almost forty years before she'd had the courage to walk away. She had stayed because of her children. Once her children had grown and left home, things really started to go downhill between her and her ex-husband. The children had been the glue that held them together.

She had dreams of travelling, and their financial situation was never to the point where they could travel far together. His idea of travelling had never matched her own. Her ex-husband was a five-star resort kind of man. Ruth did not mind five-star resorts. They were relaxing and she enjoyed the atmosphere, but she never felt like she was getting the full out-of-country experience by staying in them. Ruth was more adventurous and liked to go off the beaten path, mingle with the locals, and eat the local cuisine.

Ruth told Dusty about a trip to Jamaica she had taken the previous year where she had gone into the countryside and lived in a bamboo hut. There had been little running water, and she had lived among the local people. She had learned so much from the trip. She witnessed the struggles of the Jamaican people. She watched the homeless pick through compost piles beside the street dogs looking for something to eat. They had little, but in the evenings, there was music and dancing. They held tightly onto positive attitudes, hoping for better days ahead.

The weather in Jamaica had been so humid during the mid-afternoon. Ruth had only been able to lie on her bed in her hut and read. There was usually an afternoon downpour of rain. Most times it would be enough to fill the water storage units, so she could shower. Even in the shower, Ruth would sweat. It was an adventure she would never forget, and she knew she had grown internally from the experience.

Dusty was interested in her adventures and her travels as much as she was in his. His travels focused around trucking—things he had done in a variety of places throughout Canada and the United States while on the mandatory thirty-six-hour resets. He had friends and family all across the country. He visited festivals, NASCAR races, and events in local areas during his down time. He had spent the last twenty-seven years travelling and was well known wherever he went. He knew all the truck stops and all the highways.

He hardly ever used a map, road atlas, or GPS. He was like a human Rand McNally and was a fountain of information on all things trucking. Ruth hardly ever travelled without a GPS. It amazed her how Dusty navigated his travels in his head. His memory was remarkable. He was often consulted on routes, roads, and services by other drivers.

Ruth travelled in a different manner. Her trips took her to historical sites and different countries. While travelling with the tour, she visited cities and out-of-the-way places. It was in these out-of-the-way places that she had gained a very different perspective on the world and its people. She recognized, as she travelled with Dusty, if she were a trucker, she would do things in a very different manner than the truckers she had met. She would utilize roadside turnouts, public rest areas, and information centres.

The truck continued to roll along as Dusty chatted on the phone. Sometimes, Ruth questioned his constant connection to the Bluetooth. She hardly ever kept in touch with people while driving. She found it distracted her. She liked to focus on the landscape and scenery she was passing. Ruth enjoyed the solitude and the peace and quiet of driving alone. She enjoyed listening to her favourite music too, but most time drove in silence. She did enjoy travelling with Spencer. They shared a lot of the same interests and noticed the same things on the road.

The sun started to set, which was Dusty's cue to stop for the night. Hauling oversized and heavy haul loads restricted him to daylight hours. He was only allowed to drive from sunrise to sunset. They turned into the truck stop at Kapuskasing. Dusty stopped in the fuel line to refuel. Ruth stepped down out of the truck and walked towards the building. That was the hardest thing for Ruth; she did not want to mention her need to go to the bathroom. Stopping would delay their trip and there was so much time to be made up. A stop could take as much as fifteen to twenty minutes off their clock. It was not as easy to pull in, find a parking spot, hop out, run inside, go to the bathroom, and return to the semi as it was when she was driving in her pickup.

Dusty parked the truck and was coming in the door. Ruth was browsing around the truck stop to see what might be available to eat in the many coolers. Most of the food was prepackaged. There was a lot of deep-fried and fast foods, like chicken wings, French fries, and pizza under heat lamps. There were a variety of packaged sandwiches that looked like they had seen better days. Truck stop food did not encourage healthy eating habits. She did the best she could. She picked up raw vegetables, packaged cheese and crackers, and a banana, an orange, and an apple that were sitting in a basket next to the coffee maker.

When Ruth travelled, she ate veggie and fruit trays, single servings of berries, bananas, and pre-made salads. She would munch on the veggies and fruit as she drove.

Water was essential for her. She always strived for her fluid intake to be primarily water. She had her coffee in the morning, but from then on, she would drink water. She had not been able to drink much on the trip. Too much water caused them to stop. She had to learn to limit her intake. They found a table and started to eat. A tall, thin man approached the table. Dusty looked up, "Hey, Byron, you made it. How was your trip?"

"Good," Byron said as he slid in next to Dusty. Dusty introduced him to Ruth and then went about his conversation with Byron. Ruth sat and ate quietly. She listened to the usual conversation she had overheard many times while eating in the truck stops: complaints about dispatch, vacation drivers, other drivers, and the ways of the company. Byron concentrated on the conversation he was having with Dusty. They would be travelling together now on the way to Regina in a two-truck convoy. Ruth laughed to herself at the thought.

It was soon time for Ruth, Dusty, and Byron to return to their trucks for the night. Ruth was getting used to the tight quarters. She found it difficult to undress and stay out of Dusty's way as he settled himself for bed. He took a variety of medications before bed, and Ruth knew most of his medical problems could be solved with a healthier lifestyle. Ruth tried to stay healthy while on the road. She made a conscious effort when she was travelling.

Dusty seemed to be just the opposite. She tried to coach him and talk to him about the importance of taking better care of himself. He could make better food choices at the grocery store and walk more when he was stopped for the night. He could park further away from the truck stop entrances, too. His physical complaints were those of almost everyone in the industry and could be alleviated by being more aware of what he ate.

They crawled into the bunk and Ruth curled up in the crook of Dusty's arm as they finished making love. She enjoyed the feeling that came following their joining. Ruth thought about what was happening between them as she started to yawn. She could not help but question their infatuation with each other. Ruth was not sure whether it was the excitement of the trip or whether there was something more developing.

In the morning, Ruth realized the adventure was beginning to come to a close. Regina was only a day's drive away. Ruth knew she would soon have to say so long to Dusty and the truck. It was going to be a hard last night for her. The next day she would travel on to Edmonton with Byron, and then take the bus to Calgary. She would visit friends and Spencer to discuss the fall schedule of the tour before flying back to Nova Scotia.

The prairies came into sight as they travelled towards Winnipeg, Manitoba. Ruth was always in awe of how the open sky seemed to appear out of nowhere. It seemed like you were driving along through the trees, then, there it was, all sky and flat land as far as the eye could see. She would never tire of the view it presented.

The flatness of the prairies extended from east of Winnipeg to Calgary, Alberta. People who drove it joked about putting their vehicles on cruise control and taking a nap, there were so few bends. The grassland to Ruth was beautiful. On the west side of Winnipeg, fields of sunflowers could be seen in bloom during the fall. She looked forward to seeing them when she passed by.

Dusty began to slow down in preparation to make the turn into the truck stop where they would spend their last night together. Ruth was looking forward to seeing one of the waitresses she'd befriended a long time ago. Doris had been very accommodating one night when Ruth was trying to get something to eat after a long day on the road. The diner was only to be open for an additional fifteen minutes when Ruth arrived. Ruth had asked if she could get a sandwich to go, so she wouldn't hold up closing time.

Doris told her to sit down and enjoy a meal. Doris joined Ruth at the table and chatted with her that evening while she ate.

Ruth needed to get laundry done before leaving in the morning. She had gone through most of the clothes in her backpack. They walked into the truck stop diner. Ruth quickly scanned the room looking for Doris. She couldn't see her anywhere. Ruth sat down in a booth and picked up a menu to place her order when the waitress appeared at the table. Dusty and Byron joined her in the booth, placed their orders, and resumed their truck talk conversation.

The diner was no different than any other she had been in. There were the usual tables and chairs, booths lining the walls, and the counter where truckers could sit individually on stools. The short order cook could be seen going about his duties through the pickup window and chatted with the waitresses as they came to retrieve their orders.

Ruth lifted her head from her phone and noticed a man enter the room, stop, and look around for a place to sit. Their eyes locked when he walked towards a table slightly down from where she was sitting with Dusty and Byron. He was tall, about six foot four, and seemed to be very fit under the plaid short-sleeve shirt he was wearing. His keys jingled on the belt loop of his Levis. He was wearing work boots, and they made a quiet clop as he walked across the floor.

Ruth could not help but notice how good looking he was, and figured he was in his mid-fifties. His light brown hair was shoulder length, and his closely trimmed beard was beginning to show signs of his age. He tipped the visor of his ball cap, removed it, and sat it down on the table before sitting down to face her. He flashed her a wide smile. There was a twinkle in his eye as he winked at her. Ruth nodded to acknowledge him and smiled.

Once Ruth had finished eating, she stood up and excused herself from the table. She had laundry to do, and this would be a great place to get it done. She would do her wash and then take a shower. The laundry room was pretty quiet when she arrived. She noticed a younger, blond-haired woman sitting in the corner, reading. The woman looked up and smiled as Ruth walked in.

"There are lots of machines—no waiting tonight. My name is Gloria."

"My name is Ruth," and she started to sort and put her laundry in the machine.

"Who do you truck with?" Gloria asked, lifting her eyes from the pages of her book.

"I'm not a trucker," Ruth replied and began to tell Gloria how she came to be in Regina.

Gloria listened closely as Ruth spoke and said, "We can always use more women in the industry. I have two university degrees, but I got tired of living life in a cubicle in the corporate world, looking out the window. I took a vacation test trip with a friend of mine who suggested long-haul trucking. I went for three weeks, and, on my fortieth birthday, I quit my corporate job, went back to school, got my licence and went on the road. I have never regretted my decision."

Ruth and Gloria chatted as they did their laundry. Ruth found Gloria inspirational, and she seemed to be so content with her decision that it made Ruth wonder again if she should quit the tour and start a new career. The tour job seemed far more stressful than what she had seen while being on the road with Dusty. She had a different view of what kind of driver she would be—how she would handle things that seemed to stress out Dusty.

She would have a roof over her head, her expenses would be minimal, and her travel would be paid for. No more hustling to get a show or making sure the entertainer's expenses were covered before her own. No more having to juggle the cost of the show to ensure that everything went smoothly or that the show would go on.

In trucking, she would have a regular pay cheque she could depend on. It was her dream to be a truck driver and eventually own a small fleet. Did she dare to take the leap at fifty-eight years old? Gloria, Dusty, and Byron, along with the rest of the truckers she met, had certainly offered up food for thought. Gloria had left more of an impression on Ruth than any other person she had met on this trip.

Gloria left and Ruth proceeded to fold her laundry. She was finishing up when the man from the diner entered the laundry room with a smile on his face, "Hello again. I saw you in the diner. Is your husband a trucker?"

"Hi. I'm not married," Ruth smiled back and began to explain how she came to be sitting with Dusty and Byron.

"That is quite a story. You should go for it, if it is something you have always wanted to do. I don't know why you would want to, but it can be a great way to see the country. If you can overlook all the bullshit that comes with the job. You sound like you already have a pretty good idea about what to expect and how things work.

"My name is Gabe. I have been driving for over twenty years and I love it. The only thing that suffered was my marriage. I was never home. I have been divorced for over fifteen years. I have never found anyone who actually understands my love for the road. I see the most beautiful sunrises and sunsets. I have met great people and have enjoyed every minute of it. I don't spend a lot of time in truck stops. I usually only come in to do my laundry and take a shower. I park in turnouts with some of the most magnificent views and try to find places next to water. I like being in nature. I sometimes build a little fire to sit next to. I find it relaxes me and gives me time to think."

Ruth found herself being drawn to the man. His thoughts about trucking were much like her own. Gabe began to take his laundry from the dryer and fold it.

Once he was done, he prepared to leave. "It sure was nice talking to you. You made a very mundane chore enjoyable this evening."

He hoisted the laundry bag over his shoulder and walked towards the door. "Maybe I will see you along the road someday. The name of my truck is Mad Maxx. It's a blue W900 Kenworth. If you see it parked somewhere along the side of the road or in a truck stop, drop by. I would enjoy hearing how you made out. Until then, safe travels."

"Safe travels to you, too," and she watched him disappear out the door.

Ruth picked up her laundry, took a shower, and headed back to the truck. Dusty had disappeared. She figured he and Byron were still holed up in a corner somewhere talking shop. She got undressed and crawled in the bunk. Dusty came in and settled down beside her. They had decided only to hold each other their last night together. It was hard to be leaving the truck. She looked at the stars through the skylight of the semi and thought, "This could be my new home," and fell asleep thinking of the man she had met in the laundry room.

Morning came too soon for Ruth. She hugged and thanked Dusty over and over again for a wonderful time. It was a trip she would never forget. Their parting was hard for both of them. They had connected, both mentally and physically. As she climbed up into the cab of Byron's truck, they promised to stay in touch. When Byron pulled away from the truck stop, Ruth looked in the rear-view mirror and wondered if she would ever see or hear from Dusty again.

CHAPTER 3

Touring or Trucking

The trip to Edmonton with Byron was similar to her first day on the road with Dusty. They chatted about his family, life, and road trips. It was light and easy. Byron was as interesting as Dusty. He had his life, his past, and his thoughts on the industry. Ruth talked about her desire to truck. Byron brought up some valuable points for her to consider. He dropped her at the truck stop in Edmonton, she thanked him for the ride, and waved as he wheeled away.

She took a cab to the bus station to head to Calgary. She had a lot of thinking to do and welcomed the mindless journey of sitting on the bus and staring out the window.

When the bus stopped in Calgary, Spencer, the producer, was there to pick her up. He was tall, thin, and his long grey hair rippled in the wind. "Sure is good to see you, Ruth," he said as he walked towards her with a big smile on his face.

"Hi, Spencer. Good to see you, too. It has been quite the trip."

"Sounds like it. I have been following your excursion on social media. You sure have an adventurous spirit. I cannot wait to hear all about it."

Spencer put Ruth's backpack in the back seat. They both settled in his car and began to make their way through Calgary traffic to her hotel. Ruth chatted about her trip and the truckers she had met. It was more than obvious, by the sparkle in her eyes when she talked, she had enjoyed herself.

Spencer could see the trip had been more than she could have imagined. He began to worry she wanted to truck full time. Ruth was an extremely diligent worker and had a passion for the entertainment industry he had not seen in a long time. She worked hard, was well respected, and had been able to achieve far more than most in the past few years. A variety of professional entertainers wanted to work with her, be on her tour, and were always contacting him or her to garner spots in the show.

Ruth had her favourites she liked to work with. It was hard for another entertainer to get her attention. She had her share of upsets and disappointments in the industry. There were some who thought they knew more than she did. Seasoned entertainment professionals did not like being told what they could and could not do by a newbie. Ruth had taken it all in stride. She had a vision for what she wanted her tour to look like, and she expected those she hired to support that vision. When they did not, she graciously dismissed them from the tour and moved on to someone else.

Spencer enjoyed working with her. She put things together in such a way, it seemed easy. He had learned to trust her instincts about shows, people, and venues. They seemed to be dead on. He had come to respect her business savvy. They made a good team.

Ruth had a passion for life and adventure. She was always smiling despite some of the stresses that came with the job. She never let things get her down and always said, "Things will work out as they should." Spencer was beginning to think she had some kind of sixth sense when it came to business. He had learned to follow her lead.

She was good for him. He had not worked like this in a long time. His passion was entertainment, and he depended on her to put food on his table. The new passion he saw in her eyes began to scare him. He struggled with the idea she may leave the tour to go trucking. He hoped Ruth would come to her senses and realize, she was too old to truck. He would never find another event coordinator to do what she did or in the way she did it.

She had organized and designed three national tours in the past four years. She had worked with him for two years, learning, and then, with an unshakeable determination, started to form the bones of a national tour. "Why book little clubs and venues?" One day she looked at him and said, "Why not go national? The work involved is pretty much the same, just on a bigger scale."

Spencer had been doubtful when she first started. She was unstoppable. She worked non-stop to obtain sponsorship, then, once she had sponsorship in place, she started booking shows and mapping the route. She booked two dozen dates across the country in a couple of weeks. He was proud of her, and despite the setbacks, she was climbing the ladder at record speed. She was becoming a force to be reckoned with and was rapidly making a name for herself within the industry.

Others tried to follow what she was doing and started to try and get ahead of her, blocking her progress. She brushed it off and continued to move forward. She had worked with some of the best in the country. Everything she tried did not pan out, but she continued to try. She was determined to achieve the goals she set for herself.

Spencer respected Ruth. He was interested in more than a business relationship, but had never tried to cross the line. They both kept to themselves in hotel rooms. He did not want anything to upset the harmonious working relationship they had developed between them.

Ruth was fun. She was always smiling and up for anything. She was different from all the other women he dated. He had been divorced for years and bounced through relationships like a basketball. She kept to herself. He only knew her to have one short-term relationship since her separation. The way she talked about her trucking trip, the man she had travelled with, concerned him. She had jumped in without any hesitation at all. He could not help but feel he was starting to lose her in some way.

Spencer knew how important the trip was to her. He knew her history and love for semis and the industry. He had travelled with her enough on the road. She gravitated to big rigs with a magnetic force. She took pictures of the rigs that appealed to her. He called her a truck tourist.

She would take any opportunity to talk to the truckers. He could see the passion and titillation on her face.

It scared him and where that might leave him. Spencer dropped Ruth off at the Palliser Hotel and drove home consumed by his own thoughts. He began to realize exactly how much he would miss her, not only for business, but also in general.

Ruth checked in at the front desk and took the elevator to her floor. She unlocked the door and dropped her backpack down on the floor. She loved old hotels. This one in Calgary was one of her favourites. She was happy to be back. She loved Nova Scotia and the lifestyle it represented, but if she were ever to live in a city she would move to Calgary.

Calgary was close to the Rocky Mountains. On a clear day you could see their snow caps from Deerfoot Trail. She spent a lot of time in the Rockies and always came away feeling energized and refreshed. The mountain air was crisp and clear. The mountain trails were wonderful for hiking and led to beautiful green lakes unseen anywhere else in the country. The mountains drew her in. She spent time riding the trails on horseback and remembered a time when she had taken a trail ride with a stable company out of Banff.

The trail they took led to Fatigue Pass, an eighty-five-hundred-foot climb above sea level. It had been quite the experience for her and put all her horseback riding skills to the test. There was one point in which she was instructed to dismount the horse and walk him up the trail because the trail was so steep. If the horse slipped backwards, the guide did not have to worry about her safety. Ruth hoped to do it again someday, when she had the time.

Ruth relished the time she spent outdoors horseback riding. She had taken a few riding trips in Alberta when she had been there visiting. The trip in the Rockies she had taken alone with a guide. Spencer joined her a couple of times when she went riding in the Badlands. One afternoon, she had the pleasure of riding with a stuntwoman from the Canadian Broadcasting Corporation television series *Heartland*. The riding trails were narrow and challenging on horseback, even for Ruth, but the views when they reached the summits were spectacular.

Ruth had grown up on horseback. She received her first Shetland pony when she was three years old and was riding full-grown horses by the time she was seven. There were many falls and accidents for her, associated with horseback riding, but she always got back on. To her, horseback riding represented life in some ways. She had fallen many times and had been disappointed in parts of her life, but she had never given up.

Ruth had taken up horseback riding after a long hiatus. Following the return from her first ride in the Rockies, she realized how much she missed it. Being on horseback riding trails and enjoying what nature has to offer in the peace and tranquility of the forests was something she really missed. She started to ride whenever time allowed. Spencer had ridden in the past, just not as much as Ruth. Ruth found him to be enthusiastic and was a pleasant riding companion.

The previous summer, while the tour took the summer break, Ruth had leased a lovely, eight-year-old Arabian gelding. She spent her entire summer riding. She and

Waylon had become quite attached to one another. When the lease had expired, Ruth offered to purchase him from the owner. April had refused to sell him. Ruth walked away from the animal. She hoped in time, April would change her mind.

Ruth thought about her relationship with Spencer. He was a good man—loyal and respectful. At one time, she had given some thought to a personal relationship developing between them. Spencer was not ready for the commitment she required in a partner. She thought he would be a good one, but the many female friends he had had over time sent up a red flag. They never seemed to work out for one reason or another. He was an excellent business partner, and they worked well together. They were able to bounce ideas off one another that would benefit and further the tour.

Ruth spent many hours in the half ton with him and they had discussed many topics. She thought she knew him well, yet, there had never been a major urge to pursue anything personal with him. There seemed to be an imaginary fine line between them that neither one wanted to cross; no matter how many opportunities arose for them to do so, nothing had ever happened. Spencer was a true friend to Ruth and she valued their friendship. They flowed together too well to mix business with pleasure.

Ruth poured herself a bath and slipped into the tub, relishing in the hot water that surrounded her. Her thoughts wandered to Dusty and the relationship that had developed between them. He was unlike any man she had ever known. She wondered if she would ever hear from him again. She liked him and they had a definite connection. He was unpretentious and real. She had never known a man who worked so hard and was so good to the people around him.

He was as strong as an ox, yet, soft like well-worn shoe leather. He put on a tough appearance. Ruth knew him on a totally different level. He was like a teddy bear inside. There was something amiss about him, though. Something she could not put her finger on. She always trusted her instincts in business and when it came to people. There was something about Dusty that was just not right, despite the closeness they shared.

Since she had been separated, Ruth had always kept her distance from men and dating. She had one short rebound relationship. She got caught up in the feelings of her youth, by getting in touch with a long-lost teenage crush from high school. He was single and living in Calgary, almost thirty-five years later, and they had spent some time together. It wasn't long before they both agreed to go their separate ways. They had not been in contact for months.

He introduced her to Spencer. That was how she had become involved in the entertainment industry. Her life had really taken off since then. She had taken to the industry, and before long it occupied her every waking moment. She was good at it. She made some enemies along the way, but the good times far outweighed the stress and the negativity.

Ruth was a firm believer in things happening for a reason. People came and went in her life for a reason, too. She learned long ago, people left her life, whether on their own or because circumstances separated them. Friends who were once close were no longer in contact. She had tried to keep in touch with people, but during the past few years, her friendships had suffered because of her rigorous schedule. If she went into trucking, that would only continue.

She was happy with herself and her life now. She had finally left her husband, her children were old enough to look after themselves, and for the first time in a long time, Ruth felt free of all the responsibilities that at one time had weighed her down.

The more she thought about it, the more she began to realize it was time to give up the tour, and she began to get excited about driving a semi. She knew people would think she was crazy to give up the life and lifestyle she had developed to go trucking. Ruth did not care about what others thought of the decisions she had made for herself. She never worried about what others said about her. They were just opinions. The people who did not support her had never walked in her shoes. She continually had the philosophy that if people were not talking about her, then they were talking about someone else. She was more than happy to give the other people a break from needless gossip.

Ruth climbed out of the tub, dried herself off, yanked the robe off the back-of-the-door hook, and put it on. She opened the curtains to look out the window down onto 9th Avenue. Yes, she truly enjoyed being in Calgary, but maybe it was time for her to move on. She positioned the pillows on the bed, propped herself up to watch television, and ordered room service.

While she ate her meal of rib eye steak and baked potato, her cellphone rang.

"Hello?"

"Ruth, please," came a male voice at the other end of the line.

"This is she. Who is this?"

"Dusty, here; thought I would call and see how you made out with Byron and getting to Calgary?"

"Oh, Dusty, nice to hear from you. I made out marvellous. Byron is quite the man," she chuckled into the cellphone.

Dusty continued on telling her about what had been happening since they parted. He talked about what a wonderful time he had on the trip. He wanted to know what was happening with the tour, her, and when she thought she might be heading back to Nova Scotia.

"If I am still around in the west, maybe you can get a ride back with me," he said sounding hopeful.

Ruth filled him in on her trip. She told him she was getting settled and organized in Calgary and she was planning to fly back to Nova Scotia in a couple of days. She had a few things to do with Spencer, wanted to take a drive out to the Rockies, and then get back east. Summer was slipping away. She had not spent much time with Ambrose, and he was heading back to school. They had plans to get together and go tidal bore rafting, and she was looking forward to it.

Dusty and Ruth chatted for over an hour, and Ruth was tickled she had heard from him. She missed their conversations and found herself looking forward to seeing him again when they were both back in Nova Scotia.

Ruth's days in Calgary flew by. She spent her time connecting with old friends and business associates. Once her business was completed, she booked a day for herself to drive to Canmore and have lunch. She had a few spots she liked to visit and tried to do so every time she was in the west.

The Rockies towered above the road, and the difference in the air quality from the city to Canmore was easily detectable.

On her return to Calgary, she noticed an older model blue Kenworth sitting in a turnout. Above the windshield, in bold white letters, was the name Mad Maxx. As she drove closer, she saw a man sitting in a lawn chair backing onto the treeline. She felt her heart skip a beat. She decided to take a chance and stop to see if it was Gabe—the man she had met doing laundry in Regina.

He turned to look at the car as it came in from the highway. She slipped the car into park and opened the door, a big smile on her face. "Well, hi, there. I thought that might be you," she said getting out and walking towards him.

He stood up and started to walk towards her with a smile, "Hey, there. What are you doing out this way?"

"I ended up in Calgary after my trip and decided to take the day and drive out to Canmore before going back to Nova Scotia. There is a little restaurant I like to visit when I am out this way. I saw your truck and decided to stop."

Gabe reached into the headache rack of the Kenworth and uprooted an extra lawn chair and opened it up for her to sit down. "What are you doing out this way?" she said taking the seat he offered her.

"I'm hauling hay at the moment. I have a contract with Canadian Pacific to load and haul containers being shipped to Kentucky. Alberta has high-grade quality hay they use for the race horses down there. I go where the work is. I am an owner-operator and have been working and driving for myself for almost ten years. I can control what I haul, and when and where I want to work. I have my own schedule, and do not have to worry about deadlines for other companies and dispatchers on my back all the time to get moving. I can stop when I want, for as long as I want. I am too old to dance to the tune of a company dispatcher any longer. I like working this way better. The expenses are higher, because I have to maintain my own truck, but once you are used to it, you know what your truck is made of and what it needs. I have been driving Mad Maxx for a long time. I know what kind of condition the truck is in, and I do not worry about breaking down too much."

Ruth and Gabe sat and watched the sun go down over the Rockies from the side of Highway One. It was a beautiful late summer evening, and they chatted easily about life. Gabe told her about his broken marriage, and Ruth told him about hers. They discussed their personal lives, their future goals and plans. Gabe's thoughts on what he wanted when he was done driving were not far from her own. A small parcel of land, next to water, set in the mountains at the end of a road, somewhere away from the hustle and bustle of city life. A place in nature, where he could have a few animals, a horse or two, and live off the land.

Ruth listened as he talked and watched the expressions on his face as he described what he saw for himself when he stopped driving. "What do you want?"

Ruth smiled, "Pretty much the same thing when I am done travelling. I am not sure when that will be. I enjoy it too much to give it up right now. I have no desire to settled down anytime soon. I have been thinking about my future and retirement. That is why I am seriously considering leaving the entertainment industry and taking up trucking. I do not have many years left to put together a retirement nest egg. If I learn to drive a truck, it will give me at least six years behind the wheel. I can save and bank some money to buy a small property and retire. I, too, would like a couple of horses, a few animals, and to be next to water. I am not sure where that will be, yet. I have seen some beautiful country. It will be hard to decide where I want to settle when I decide to retire. I have an idea of what I want, not where I want it, if that makes sense?"

"It makes perfect sense. I feel the same way, sometimes. I really like it on the east coast of the country, but I really enjoy being in the west, too. It is hard to think about settling down and exactly where I want to do that."

"I always dreamed of driving a truck, owning my own, and then maybe starting a small business. I am not sure if that will pan out for me now. I am beginning to lean towards trying."

"I think you should, if it is something you have always wanted to do. If you can, why not? If you go through the course and do not like it when you are done, you will have done it and know for sure. This way, you continue to dream, and if you do not do it, who knows, you may regret it in the future."

Ruth got up to leave and folded the chair. "You know, you are right. Thanks for the conversation. I sincerely enjoyed the evening. I have to get back to the city. I have an early flight in the morning. I sure am glad I ran into you today. I am going to give you my cellphone number. Keep in touch, if you like. It would be good to hear from you from time to time."

Ruth wrote down her personal cellphone number and handed it to him. He quickly jotted down his on a piece of paper he slipped from his pocket and handed it to her. "Yes, stay in touch. Let me know if you decide to take the course. You have my full support, and if there is anything you need to know or I can help you with, do not hesitate to call. I would be happy to help in any way I can."

Ruth walked back to her rental car and got in. Before she moved the car, she punched his phone number into her cellphone contacts list. She beeped the horn, waved, and pulled out onto the highway.

Ruth called Spencer when she got back to the city and told him she was going to take a few weeks off to try and figure out what she wanted to do. The shows for fall were lined up. Everything that could be done until a week or so before show nights were done. The only thing Spencer would have to do while she was taking the hiatus was continue to promote and monitor social media. She would handle any inquiries via email. She would be working very little while she took the time off to decide what she wanted to do.

Spencer knew by the sound of her voice she was struggling with whether she wanted to continue with the tour or go and live her dream of trucking. He had a feeling he would be losing her to the trucking industry. He hoped he would hear back from her that she had decided to stay with the tour. As he hung up the phone, he knew deep down, she would be leaving the entertainment industry. Trucking was her passion, and he could see she would be going on another adventure. He would miss her.

CHAPTER 4
Back to School

R uth boarded the flight for Halifax. She usually flew the red eye and slept most of the way. She had not been able to get a seat for the overnight flight. Taking the day flight, she would settle down with work to pass the time. She would take a much-needed vacation when she landed. She did not want to think about the tour. She wanted to think about her future.

She had been talking to Dusty off and on and he seemed as interested as ever. He was excited she had decided to take a look at trucking. He had offered to take her out on as many trips as she wanted and looked forward to travelling with her. He was more than willing to help her, introduce her to his boss at R.A.E., and put in a good word for her. He seemed to be as excited as she was.

He began calling and texting her all the time. They would spend hours on the phone. Ruth was beginning to feel overwhelmed with the attention he was showering her with. Sometimes, it seemed suffocating. Ruth had never been pursued by any man like Dusty. She began to find herself being wrapped up in his affection. She awoke every morning to a text of "Good Morning, Gorgeous." It felt good to have a man in her life who seemed so interested in having a relationship with her.

He was soon talking about how he could see a future for them. They discussed team driving, owning their own truck, and eventually opening a company and starting to build a small fleet. He talked to her about the business aspect of the industry. What she may have to learn, deal with, how to get business, how to hire and handle drivers. He discussed his property in Newfoundland, and how he wanted to develop it. It would be big enough for what she said she wanted, a couple of horses, next to the ocean. She would be able to get up in the morning, have her coffee on a veranda overlooking the water. She could live a quiet life, relax, and do whatever she wanted to do.

Ruth found herself dreaming about a future with him. She started looking at him as a full-time partner and what it would be like living with him on a permanent basis. She could wake up next to him on the trip, but what about all the time? He would have to continue to work and drive. If she started to truck, she would be on the road. They would not be travelling in the same truck. They would end up meeting like other driving couples—in truck stops, on their way either coming or going or whenever the opportunity arose.

Most long-haul truckers only had two or three days at home a month. Was this the kind of relationship she wanted? She would need someone in her life she could trust completely. Was this the case with Dusty? She still had that nagging suspicion in the back of her mind that he was holding something back. She could not put her finger on it, but she could not shake the feeling, either.

She certainly had not been looking or thinking about a permanent relationship until Dusty. He seemed to drop in from nowhere and take over her heart. She had a hard time trying to figure out what it was about him that attracted her to him. It seemed with Dusty, she had thrown all caution to the wind and was swiftly falling in love with a man who had come out of nowhere.

When the plane landed in Halifax, Ruth disembarked and went to the baggage claim, picked up her backpack, and walked towards the exit. Ambrose was waiting for her when she came out. She was thrilled to see him. She and he were closer than she was with Abby. Abby carried a chip on her shoulder when it came to Ruth. Ruth had long accepted that Abby would come around on her own terms eventually.

Abby resented Ruth for leaving her father and did not understand, even at the age of thirty-four, why Ruth and her father were no longer together. Abby had a vision of what their family was like, and the way things had fallen apart were not part of Abby's vision. Ruth tried to help her understand she no longer loved Abby's father. They were friends. They would never be able to repair the forty years of damage that had occurred between them.

Ambrose rattled on about his summer, his new girl-friend, and what he had been doing since Ruth had left on her trucking adventure. She enjoyed hearing him talk and seeing how excited he was about his future. Ambrose had taken his divorce hard and had taken a long time in getting his life together once he returned home. Now, he was back in school and dating a lovely young woman Ruth liked and he was excited about life. She hoped the positive turn of events meant a bright and prosperous future for him.

There was a time not too long ago that Ruth would not have considered leaving him on his own after his divorce. Now, he was upbeat and jovial about his future. She felt more comfortable leaving him and going about her own life. She told him about her idea of leaving the entertainment industry and getting her trucking licence. Ambrose was supportive of her idea, as long as she was sure it was what she wanted to do. He was behind whatever she was doing as long as she was happy doing it.

Ruth dropped him off at his apartment and went home. It seemed like forever since she had been there. It felt good to be back in her own space. She dropped her backpack at the door and went into the bedroom to change into something more comfortable. She walked to the kitchen and opened the fridge to see what was there. She had not eaten in a while and her stomach began to complain about being ignored. There was not much, but she was able to put together some cheese and crackers along with a bowl of soup. It would have to do until she could get out to the grocery store in the morning.

She was not home long when Dusty called. He was in constant contact with her. She chatted with him for a bit and hung up. She needed some space to think things through and decide what she wanted to do. Her chance meeting with Gabe along the side of the highway had given her more to think about. His encouragement seemed to mean more to her than all the attention that came from Dusty.

Ruth spent the next couple of weeks disconnected from work, social media, and her friends. She spent her time researching the trucking industry and the requirements necessary to get into school. She researched the different schools and options the trucking companies offered.

There were companies that offered the Free Way Program, where they held training classes at their company headquarters. You attended for free and then signed a two-year contract requiring you to drive with them for a two-year period.

Ruth visited company offices and sat down with their Human Resources departments to discuss her entry into school and into the industry. She finally settled on a school and attended a meeting with the Admissions Officer. Terry was encouraged at her enthusiasm and passion to become a truck driver. He immediately welcomed her into the program. Ruth paid the admission fee and booked her seat. She was not sure if it was exactly what she wanted to do, but at least she had a spot. She could back out if she wanted, but for now, she walked out of the office feeling like she had wings.

She talked to Dusty that afternoon and told him she had registered for the Class One program. He was going to Newfoundland and invited her to come along for the trip. It would be good to see him again. She had been to Newfoundland a couple of times. This trip would give her an opportunity to visit a long-time friend and further explore the island.

She packed her backpack, made a couple of phone calls, and before she knew it, she was sitting in the passenger seat of the Freightliner bouncing over the pavement towards the Newfoundland Ferry. She and Dusty decided to get a cabin for the overnight crossing. As a trucker, he was entitled to a bunk in a four-bunk cabin. The truckers did not get rooms to themselves unless they upgraded their company passage fare. Female truckers were treated the same, unless there was only one female trucker on the ferry, then she had a cabin to herself.

Dusty and Ruth yearned to be together and booked a cabin to themselves. The ferry left the dock and it was not long before they were naked in the bunk wrapped in each other's arms. The ferry rolled with the waves at almost the same rhythm as their lovemaking. They fell asleep and did not wake up until the announcement they were one hour away from docking in Channel-Port aux Basque.

They got up, showered, and dressed. They arrived downstairs just in time to return to the truck. Dusty started the truck and they exited the ferry, stopped for coffee, and proceeded on the Trans-Canada Highway towards Stephenville.

Josh was parked at Wal-Mart waiting to meet Ruth. Dusty kissed her and hugged her tight as he handed her over to Josh in the parking lot. Josh and Ruth had been roommates over thirty years ago and had remained friends.

"I will be out of cellphone range for a few days. I will be going home to visit my mother after I make my drop. Cellphone service is not available there. I will be in touch as soon as I can," he said as he climbed up into the driver's seat and closed the door.

Ruth and Josh spent the next few days catching up on each other's news. Ruth told Josh she had tried relentlessly to bring the tour to Newfoundland, but had never been able to secure a show. It was expensive for venues to have entertainers visit the island, and there were few who would pay to do so. Newfoundland was filled with an array of entertainers. The entertainers who were paid to visit were ones that would fill stadiums or concert halls. Every tour, Ruth continued to try and secure a show on the island.

"Why don't you take my car and go across the island and see if you can book a show here. I know, you're planning to give it up, but as you are here, you may as well give it try before you're done with the tour."

"I think, I will. Maybe I will drop down around Dusty's hometown and surprise him. I would not go to his mother's. I could stay in a hotel close by and see him in between. I can stop along the way and try and get a couple of shows. Kill two birds with one stone, so to speak."

Ruth packed up her things the next morning and started out on the road for St. John's. She had never been that far across the island. She was looking forward to seeing the country between Stephenville and St. John's. She had been to the St. John's Airport as a stopover to England when she went to visit Abby, but had not seen the landscape across the island.

As she motored along, she was in awe of the scenery and how diverse it was. The landscape was peppered with rocks and barren land. The Trans-Canada Highway led through small towns, larger urban areas, and vast wilderness. Ruth noted the many moose warning signs that appeared almost nonstop. She stopped at a variety of lookout points and marvelled at the breathtaking views. She was especially taken with the expanse of birch trees that lined the road for miles through Green Bay. She stopped in Gander, Grand Falls-Windsor, and met with a variety of venues in hopes of procuring a show. At the end of the day, she stopped for the night close to Goobies, in anticipation of changing her direction south in the morning towards Marystown and Burin.

The next morning, when she arrived in Marystown, she would give Dusty a call. She was hoping he would join her. When she arrived, she dialed his number and left a message on his voicemail. She started looking for venues and driving around the area.

It was a beautiful day, and the small town in which he lived was scenic, and there was a relaxed feel about it. As she waited to hear from him, she met with a variety of people in Marystown, Burin, and the surrounding areas. Those she met seemed very interested, and Ruth was hoping to bring the tour to Dusty's community. She visited local historical sites, and spent the day resting and relaxing.

Finally, upon her return to the hotel room, the phone rang. "Hey, there. I am in your area looking for a venue for a show and thought if you have some time we might get together."

"I would love to. But I am not there anymore. I was called out to go to Labrador and left at four o'clock this morning."

"Oh, that's too bad. I think, it would have been fun. What a beautiful area you live in."

"Maybe next time. I have to go. I will call you in a couple of days to tell you when I will be back in Stephenville to pick you up."

Ruth hung up the phone and began to gather her things to check out. She would take as much of the coastal roads as possible for her return to Stephenville, and she would return to stay with Josh until she heard from Dusty. It was a sunny afternoon, and Ruth enjoyed the leisurely pace. She rolled down the windows, turned on her Spotify, and sang along to the tunes while a warm breeze blew through the car.

She drove past some of the most spectacular landscape Mother Nature could produce. Newfoundland was one of the most picturesque provinces she had ever been in. The landscape was unlike any she had seen—all in one place. There were rocks, barren land, mountains, and flat prairie land. There was water everywhere. The secondary road took her through small fishing villages and along shorelines decorated with wharves, fish houses, and fishing boats.

Newfoundland was an array of rugged coastlines, pounding surf, and sporadic barren land. It had a wild feel to it. It would be quite the province to drive through in a semi, she thought. The Wreckhouse region was famous for being a dangerous spot when the winds were high. Many trucks had been blown over when drivers tried to tackle the piece of highway, in spite of the wind warnings that were issued. There always seemed to be one or two truckers who ignored the warnings and decided they could make it through. Some did, some did not, and a lot did not take the chance.

Ruth finally received a call from Dusty. He would be picking her up the next day. She was anxious to see him and tell him all about what she had seen in his area and how much she had enjoyed her time there. She and Josh walked the beaches, hiked the trails, and went horseback riding. They had been able to catch up on the many years since they had last seen each other. She was ready to return home, continue her research, and prepare for leaving the tour and going back to school. She knew in her heart this was the right thing for her to do, and she could not wait to get started.

CHAPTER 5

Following a Dream

The next few months were busy ones. She was on the road with Dusty while trying to clean up details with the fall tour schedule. She had agreed to stay on until the last show. She would not be there for it, but she would finish her duties as Event Coordinator. She would make sure everything was in place so the show would be a success. Spencer was grateful she was going to stay on until he found another person to replace her.

Ruth kept in close touch with Spencer as the fall tour schedule began its run. She was going to have to cancel one show, owing to lack of interest. There was too much going on in the town to accommodate another entertainment choice. Ticket sales were slow. Another planned show was going well, and the last one was coming together nicely.

She was ready to start classes at the end of February. It was perfect timing. She could continue to travel with Dusty in the truck to learn, and be home with Ambrose during the holiday season. She could finish up the tour for the year, and then make her way to Sydney where she was enrolled in the Class One program.

She travelled with Dusty at every opportunity. Their destinations included Ontario, Newfoundland, Tennessee, Georgia, North and South Carolina, and all the places in between. She was learning, helping out with paperwork, and doing pre-trip inspections. She was inputting all the information into the ELD and was getting skilled in how it worked.

She was helping to chain down the machines and was getting better at using the binders, straps, and ratchets. Dusty would laugh almost uncontrollably as he watched her dangle from the winch bar trying to make sure the load was secure.

Dusty usually hauled decks and floats, but on an upcoming trip to Tennessee, he would be hauling a refrigeration unit. In the industry, it was referred to as a reefer. It was a temperature-controlled unit. Whatever went in could be kept cool for transport. Reefers were primarily used for hauling produce, fish, ice cream, and meat products. They could also be used for products that required a constant temperature to remain in their present state. Ruth was anxious to see how it worked.

The two of them continued to have fun when they travelled together. They were getting to know the little things about one another. There did not seem to be anything that bothered or annoyed them. Ruth chuckled at Dusty's little quirks. She chalked her tolerance up to travelling extensively with professional entertainers.

Dusty seemed to be getting used to having a travelling companion in the truck, and he missed her when she was not with him. She enjoyed riding in the cab and the schedule they were keeping. The weather, most of the time, was sunny, and Ruth had a wonderful time sitting in the passenger seat taking pictures and marvelling at the countryside as they passed by. More than once during the winter months, she was amazed by Dusty's winter driving skills. Snow blew around the truck, and the roads were ice covered. Ruth and Dusty hardly spoke during these times, as Dusty had to have full concentration on the highway.

They spent their evenings in each other's arms. They chatted and caressed each other until they fell into a natural body rhythm of their lovemaking. It ended with both of them spent, curled up together, and falling asleep. They seemed to be a natural fit.

She sat one evening on a return trip home in the sunroom with her girlfriend Cindy relaying the events that had unfolded since she had met Dusty. Cindy was thrilled for her; it had been a long time since she had seen Ruth this happy.

Ruth told Cindy there was something nagging at her about him, but she could not put her finger on it. Cindy told Ruth she was overthinking things. Cindy told her to relax and enjoy the relationship for what it was, and to stop looking for something that was more than likely not there. The rest would work itself out. Ruth wanted to put her anxiety aside, but she could not help wondering if there was something she was missing.

Cindy and Ruth continued to chat, and Ruth mentioned Dusty said his late father was an entertainer and quite well known in Newfoundland. Cindy was originally from Newfoundland and could not remember ever hearing his name.

Ruth and Cindy decided to Google Dusty's father's obituary and see what it said about the late singer. They sat and scrolled through the information together. Ruth caught her breath. There it was, what had been nagging at her. Dusty, as of a year ago, had a significant other. He resided a significant distance from his hometown. Things started to fall together and make sense. Ruth looked at the name of the woman and referred to Facebook to see if she could find out further information.

Ruth scrolled through the woman's Facebook account. There were recent pictures of her and Dusty together. Ruth sat dumbfounded and stared at the pictures. How could he do this? Ruth downloaded one of the pictures and sent it in a text to Dusty with the words, "Is there something I should know?"

There was no return message. Ruth sent Dusty another text telling him she was at Cindy's and would contact him again when she got home. Cindy speedily came to Dusty's defence and told Ruth not to jump to conclusions. "It does look suspicious. Wait until you talk to him. They may not be together now, and she just hasn't taken the pictures down."

Ruth agreed to give Dusty the benefit of the doubt. "It doesn't look good though, Cindy. It all seemed too good to be true. Why would he do this?"

Ruth finished her visit with Cindy and started home. Her head was reeling with everything she had seen that night, and tears streamed down her cheeks. She was anxious to discuss it all with Dusty. Ruth settled herself down, picked up her cellphone, and dialed his number.

"Hello. How was your visit with Cindy?" he said in a sheepish voice.

"It was fine until I saw the pictures. Are you going to tell me about her, and why you would lie to me for so long?"

Dusty began to explain about his female partner of four and a half years, how their relationship was on the rocks. He had been ready to leave her for a long time. He met Ruth and everything changed for him. He was in love with her and would tell Loretta. "I'm going to leave her as soon as I get back to Newfoundland."

Ruth listened carefully to what he had to say. She wanted to believe him. They had such a great relationship. She was baffled by the way he'd kept Loretta a secret from her. She told him, she needed time to think things through. She was not sure what she wanted to do.

"Give me a chance to make things right. I do not want to lose you," Dusty said with desperation in his voice.

Ruth was going to be busy getting ready to move to go to school. The Christmas holidays were soon coming and Dusty would be going home. She would not be seeing him until after the new year. She would let it lay and see what happened.

The relationship between Ruth and Dusty was strained. They continued to talk on the phone and keep in touch. Dusty continued to reassure Ruth he was going to leave as soon as he could. Ruth continued half-heartedly to believe him. She was far too busy to worry about what was going on with Dusty and his life.

New Year's Eve came and went in a quiet evening at home for Ruth. She was getting settled in her new apartment in Sydney. She made herself a nice Italian dinner, opened a bottle of red wine, and sat back surveying her new surroundings. She was secretly hoping she would hear from Dusty in some way, but as the midnight countdown came and went, she finished her wine and went to bed.

Ruth got up bright and early her first day of school. As she sat in her half ton in the school's parking lot, she looked around her and watched as men and women of all ages filed through the doors. She opened her door, took a deep breath, slung her backpack over her shoulder, and walked across the parking lot to the entrance.

There was an introduction meeting, where she was informed of the school policies. She had to sign an agreement with the school for attendance and attitude towards classes and fellow classmates. She had butterflies in her stomach. She was the only woman in the class. The other five students were young men who looked to be in their twenties and early thirties. She smiled to herself as she looked around. These young men were all younger than Ambrose. "It is a good thing I get along with kids," she thought.

Getting used to school was quite an endeavour for Ruth. She lived such a different life from getting up early, making her lunch, coming home, and studying. Her previous job had been late nights, long days behind the wheel, a whirlwind of shows, people, different places, and planning the next travel route. Even with the previous months of being in the truck, it was still travelling, meeting new people, and seeing new places.

Ruth found it hard to get into a regular routine and would often wonder if she was making the right choice. When thoughts of doubt would enter her mind, something would happen to bring her back and help her realize this was what she really wanted to do.

She had lost a lot of friends when she started school. The entertainers from the tour stopped contacting her. They moved on to other agents. She was no longer useful to them. They had been concerned about their pay cheques and what she was doing to help them increase it. Now that she was no longer in the business, they no longer contacted her.

Some of them stuck around, but their contact became sporadic, and eventually she received no phone calls from anyone in the entertainment industry. Spencer no longer called her to see how she was doing or to check in. She sometimes missed the entertainment industry, but, more and more, the prospect of driving a truck full time brought a new kind of excitement to her day.

Her age did not seem to matter to the young men in the class. She was old enough to be their mother, and in some cases their grandmother. They were getting used to her sense of humour and were finding her mindset was far younger than the age on her birth certificate.

The young men frustrated her. She tried not to let it bother her. She tried to focus completely on driving and school work. Dusty called almost every day and most times chatted easily on the phone. Some calls were rattled with discussions about what was going to happen. Ruth wanted closure to his current relationship. He seemed to be dragging his feet when it came to leaving Loretta. There were no longer conversations about their future, what was going to happen, and when he planned to return to his present home and retrieve his belongings.

Ruth tried not to let it consume her. She tried to stay focused on her driving and her future. She knew there was nothing she could do about it and tried not to put pressure on him. He became defensive and upset when she tried to talk to him about it. She was learning how to let it lay and tried to keep her head in the game of school.

Ruth settled into a good study routine. She had been good in school, and academics came easily to her. Her marks were high, and she was happy with the results. She was the only student in her class to pass the air brakes exam on the first writing.

Driving was another challenge she was trying to overcome. She had driven an automatic all her life, and getting used to the thirteen-speed gear shift of the semi presented a whole new challenge to her driving skills. She struggled with the clutch and the gear shift, making sure she was in the right gear for the right speed, and timing her shifts properly.

She found it difficult to judge her distance when making turns. She and the curb were becoming quite good friends. There were days she could not shift, and the sounds emitting from the grinding of the transmission were those of pure pain. At times, she thought the transmission would drop right in the middle of the road.

She narrowly avoided light standards, stop signs, and vehicles parked on the sides of streets when she misjudged the turn. There were times her instructor had to slam on the emergency brake pedal that was positioned on the passenger floor to ensure she did not hit anything. She had stalled the truck in the middle of intersections, as she struggled to make sure she was in the right gear and to slow down.

Her instructors were caring, understanding, and patient beyond what Ruth could even fathom. She had respect for their ability to sit in the passenger seat while untrained students tried to manoeuvre these huge road ships through the city. Ruth knew she would not have been able to do what they did.

Ruth was determined to conquer the truck, and all that came with it, to become the very best driver she could. Every day things seemed to get a bit easier, and as time went on, she saw large improvements in her ability to shift the gears. She was now in a position to concentrate solely on the trailer and to learn where and when to turn in the intersections. She realized backing the huge machine did not seem to be as hard as she would have thought. She knew when she delivered to loading docks around the country, that might not be the case.

The first time she had attempted to back it in had gone well. Beginner's luck, she thought. She struggled with the task almost every time thereafter. She knew she would eventually get the hang of it and she would improve the more practice she received. She chuckled to herself thinking about the warehouse employees who would be standing on the sidelines laughing at the woman trying to back the semi in.

Her instructors were two very different types of men. Dave was about sixty years old and was relaxed and easy going. He was encouraging and instrumental in showing her if you put your mind to it, you can achieve anything.

Warren was a different type of man altogether. He was much younger than Ruth and would be the tester for her licence. When she had first started driving with him, she just shook her head and tried to get a grasp of his teaching style. He was aggressive, always on her case, and did not let even the slightest error go unnoticed. He frustrated her and made her almost give up. There had been days she had stopped driving and told him to take the wheel, that she was unable to continue.

As Ruth spent more time with him in the truck, she realized his way of teaching was one of genuine concern for her as a driver and for others on the road. She knew when she received her Class One licence from him, she would deserve it. He was about trucking safety and making her draw, from within herself, the best possible driver she could be. Ruth found herself wanting to do the same, and his determination to help her succeed only gave her more determination to do so.

She chatted with a couple of truckers online and on the phone. Most were young men, and their banter and comments made her smile. She had been used to a variety of comments from men when she had been travelling with the musicians, and her sense of humour was quick with comebacks. They were supportive, and they were helpful when she had questions. She looked forward to meeting more women on the road when she was travelling. She had mainly encountered the men in the industry.

Ruth had been in touch with Gloria, the woman she had met in Regina. Gloria was thrilled for her when she told her she was taking the course. "That's awesome. You'll be a great truck driver. Keep me posted on how you are doing," Gloria told her with enthusiasm

As the course weeks went by, Ruth became more and more proficient at shifting gears and was pleased with her progress. Dave and Warren had taken her out for a couple of days for extra practice, and she was grateful for the opportunities they were giving her. She had the feeling that Warren was interested in more than just teaching her how to drive, but she put those thoughts aside and continued to focus on her driving.

Before she knew it, the course was winding down and there were only three weeks left. Ruth was surprised the time had gone so quickly. She was amazed at how well she had done. She was concerned about passing the road test, but had been reassured she was progressing at the standard rate and she would be fine.

Even if she did not pass, she knew she could do it again and would eventually become a truck driver. She would realize her dream. She loved driving the truck, and the days that took her onto the highway for driving practice were some of the best days for her. The instructors recognized her love for the open road and were always happy to accommodate her by taking her out on the highway when the week was winding down for the weekend. They knew for Ruth it would end her week on a good note.

Ruth was getting better at mastering the thirteen-speed gear shift of the International she was driving. She and Warren had a lot of disagreements when she was behind the wheel. She found he was beginning to irritate her. She started to make numerous mistakes and could not seem to concentrate. He continually pointed out each tiny error, and endlessly nagged her about whatever he could. Ruth started to think it may have something to do with her being a woman behind the wheel.

Things were different with her male classmates. Driving days, students were taken out to practice in pairs. Each student had a specific amount of time behind the wheel. Ruth started to take notes about how Warren treated and spoke to the young men while they were driving, as compared to how he was directing and talking with her. There was no doubt in her mind there was a different kind of lesson delivery between her and the other (male) students.

She met with the school's administration and advised them of her findings. She told them she would no longer be able to learn or drive with Warren. She wanted to continue her driver training with Dave.

They granted her request and understood her complaints. There had been many females who had complained before her. Ruth was sure there would be many more, if he did not change his teaching ways. Road test day approached. Ruth was anxious about taking the road test with Warren.

The day before the final road test, Ruth had her pre-test day. Dave's job would be to sit in the passenger seat and not say a word, other than direct her around town and where he wanted her to go. When the practice road test was completed, they returned to the school yard. "Just do the same thing tomorrow and you will be fine. Take your time; you will have all morning," Dave told her before she left for the rest of the day.

The morning dawned rainy and damp. It was the very first day it had rained while Ruth was doing her driving course. She looked out the window and chuckled. Rain falls on the lucky, she thought. She grabbed her backpack and headed out the door of her apartment.

Warren was late getting to the yard. Ruth waited patiently for his arrival. She was more nervous than she thought she would be. She wondered how she was ever going to get through the morning and pass the test.

They went over the pre-trip inspection and the air brake inspection. Warren had to tell her to relax and slow down. "Get your act together," Ruth thought to herself. She could not seem to think properly. Her mind went blank as she tried to walk herself through the pre-trip and air brake inspections. Ruth took a deep breath, blocked out everything around her, and started from the beginning. The information flowed once she focused.

They drove around the city so Ruth could relax. Ruth went about the road test as if she were doing her job. She blocked Warren out and drove through the streets, making the turns and following the routes she had taken so many times before. She finished up by backing up and parking in one of the local trucking company yards. Warren sat and went over the test with her. She passed, and he signed her licence.

Ruth was overcome with relief when the test was over, and he passed over the piece of paper that indicated she had earned her Class One licence. "Thank you. You will not regret signing these, I promise," she said with tears streaming down her face.

"Let me drive you back to the school yard. I figure you have had enough driving for today." Ruth could not believe it was all over. She called Dusty to let him know she had passed. "I knew you could do it. I'm so proud of you," he said.

Ruth sat in her little apartment and looked around. So much had changed for her over the past few months—the way she thought, what she found important, and how she looked at things. Life seemed to be taking such a dramatic turn for her, and she was happy with the changes.

As part of the course, there was a four-week internship with a trucking company driving coach to complete the requirements to receive her graduation certificate. Dusty had already approached R.A.E. about her travelling with him for the internship and continuing the education he taught her before she went to school. They had agreed to her training and were more than interested in her working for the company once she had graduated. Ruth was thrilled, and was looking forward to being back on the road with Dusty.

While making their internship plan, she was upfront with Dusty about what she expected before she would get in the truck with him. She knew what the opportunity meant for her future. She tried to focus on what she needed to do instead of the personal relationship between them. It was one of the reasons Ruth had never liked to mix business with pleasure. She knew that with the different situations that can arise in a personal relationship, the business details suffer.

Dusty seemed to be back peddling about being her coach. He had to meet with the school and do a course. The company still wanted Ruth, but she may have to go with another driving coach. It sounded to Ruth that he might be trying to pawn her off on another company trainer. Dusty denied it.

She talked to Dave a little bit about the Internship Program and the problems she might have in working with Dusty and R.A.E. Trucking. He told her he would be able to arrange a different route for her, should she need it. Ruth was grateful for his assistance and tried to put her worries aside and trust things would work out for her. They had so far, so she was trying to continue to hold out hope.

Dusty's stuff was still at his house in Newfoundland, and there had been no talk of his situation changing anytime soon. He continued to stay with Ruth whenever he was in the city. They continued their relationship as if he had already moved out.

Ruth tried to rationalize their relationship by thinking he spent far more time with her than he did going to where the majority of his belongings were, and she was looking forward to being on the road with him for her Internship.

Now, with the academics and driver training portion of the course finished, Ruth waited for word she would be leaving with Dusty to do the four-week Internship needed to receive her graduation certificate.

She had been back to visit friends and say her goodbyes to her old life. She had visited with Connie and Dorothy. It could be a very long time before she saw them again. She visited with her sister and her friends. She spent as much time with Ambrose as she could. He had graduated from trade school the week after Ruth had gotten her licence. Ruth had been so proud of him the day he walked across the stage.

Things had changed so much for Ruth over the course of her training, and she was anxious to get started on the final weeks of her internship. It was not long before the call came from Dusty telling her she would be leaving. She packed her bags with her safety and work gear, some extra clothes, and was off to join Dusty in the Freightliner.

Ruth arrived at the yard to load her stuff in the first big rig she had ever driven. She had moved it around the yard one night after Dusty returned from being away. She had butterflies in her stomach as she hoisted her bags and belongings up onto the passenger seat of the truck. She was not sure how Dusty was going to handle sitting in the passenger seat. He was a driver. R.A.E. had entered her driving information into the ELD system. She slid behind the wheel, adjusted her mirrors and seat, entered the required driver information into the system, and then looked at Dusty.

"Are you ready?" he said with a twinkle in his eye.

"Are you ready?" she laughed as she turned the key and shifted the truck into first gear.

The truck eased ahead. Ruth shifted up and down as needed to gain and reduce speed until they got out onto the highway. They chatted and laughed about her mistakes and her grinding of the gears. She battled with the stick shift to find the appropriate gear. "I am going to call you Rookie Grinder," Dusty laughed.

Ruth drove along listening to the radio as Dusty filled his time chatting on the phone with the other drivers and making jokes about her skills. He did not seem at all nervous, and corrected and helped when she needed his attention. She drove for most of the day and pulled into the truck stop in Salisbury, New Brunswick, where they would be spending the night. She and Dusty went over her mistakes and discussed where she could improve.

Their days were pretty much the same as when he was driving. It was different for her to be behind the wheel. She drove most of the trip. Dusty had to take the wheel when they were pressed by dispatch, so her driving hours were interrupted on occasion, but the hours did continue to accumulate as their schedule allowed.

They talked little of his relationship status with Loretta. When they did, it resulted in arguments that ended with both of them stressed and upset. Ruth was unable to concentrate on her driving when these arguments happened. She had started refusing to drive, and Dusty would take the wheel. She would sit in the passenger seat, listen to music, and watch the landscape go by without even looking at him.

The silence in the truck during these times was deafening. Ruth continued to battle herself and question what she was doing in this relationship with Dusty. She continued in order to complete her internship and graduate from school, but there were times she even questioned herself whether it was worth the agony of what she was going through personally to achieve what she wanted to achieve.

Dusty could be impatient with her and she became very aware there was so much more she could have learned in school. Her backing up skills were sketchy, she had no experience with night time driving, and a lot of the time, her shifting was rough. Dispatch was always on their case about getting to the customer on time, and Ruth found herself struggling with not being good enough to perform the job. She questioned many times whether this was actually the job for her and whether she should go back to being an event coordinator.

During some of their arguments, she threatened more than once to quit and go home. She struggled with the private conversations Dusty had with Loretta on the phone. She was forced to wait for him to finish before she could return to the truck, or she had to wait for him to return to the truck once he finished talking to her.

She tried to remain positive and kept telling herself she could do this. The guys from R.A.E. with whom Dusty talked to on the phone continually made jokes about her skills. There were some who offered up encouragement to keep going.

Loretta was a real thorn in Ruth's side. Dusty had not revealed to her that Ruth was in the truck, and Ruth continually thought, if he would lie to Loretta then what was keeping him from lying to her. Ruth tried to put their personal relationship aside as she made her way through traffic on Highway 401 and through the streets of Toronto.

The loads she was hauling were a variety of items. There were rock screeners, transformers, excavators, and many different items housed in vans and reefers. Ruth enjoyed hauling the oversized and heavy-haul loads. There was more of a challenge to it. She was like a kid in a candy store when the time came to load and chain down the machinery. She had to drive the excavator onto the float and had a great time moving the controls of the big machine as Dusty directed her on which way to move the joy sticks.

It was a beautiful sunny day, and Ruth was rolling down the 401 heading for Toronto when her one-hundred-hour alarm went off on her cellphone. Ruth had set it to indicate when she had reached her one hundred hours of driving time needed to graduate. She took a camera shot of the odometer and pulled into the truck stop at Napanee. She jumped out of the truck, did a little happy dance in the parking lot, and told Dusty she was not going to drive any more that day. "Today is my graduation day. Today, I am done driving and have to celebrate this milestone in my life," she said with a big smile on her face.

Dusty laughed and agreed to take the wheel. Ruth was grinning from ear to ear as they pulled back out onto the highway to continue the trip. He was proud of her and all she had accomplished. He wanted her to be able to relax and enjoy the moment that came with her graduating.

They parked the truck in the yard in Bolton, Ontario, and Ruth climbed down and started to make a few phone calls letting people know she had finally graduated. She was excited and extremely proud of herself. Dusty had stopped and picked up a bottle of wine and steaks to barbeque for supper to try and make the day even more special for her. Their schedule did not make it easy to take the time to celebrate special occasions. He was determined to do the best he could.

They sat on an empty float in the yard after their meal enjoying a drink together. They chatted about the future and what they both expected from their relationship. They danced around the topic of Loretta and what he was planning to do when he went home. Ruth was getting tired of the same old story and how, after all this time, he had failed to make a decision.

Ruth tried to put it out of her mind as she climbed in the truck to get ready for bed. Dusty was close behind her and he positioned himself on his side facing her and drew her into him. His hands began to wander over her body, caressing her, and he lightly pinched her erect nipples. He took her breast in his hand and kneaded it. She began to moan with pleasure as he raised himself above her to take the nipple into his mouth. She ran her hands over his back and down over his buttocks, giving them a playful slap. She could feel his erection growing and the warmth of the wine she drank began to build up inside of her.

He took her body in his arm and swung her underneath him. Looking into her eyes, he started to pepper her with small feathery kisses down her neck, over her breast, and over her belly, the stubble from his unshaven face brushing her skin on the way down. His hot tongue licked lightly at her bare mound, and as he spread her legs, her body shuddered with pleasure and desire.

He continued to cover her with little kisses as he moved back up over her belly and breasts to her lips. His kiss was passionate and overwhelming. Ruth began to repeat Dusty's previous motions, moving down to his rock-hard cock that was standing erect between his legs. She took it into her mouth, relaxed her throat muscles, and let it slide back into the depths of her mouth. Overtaken by the sensation that was enveloping his body, Dusty struggled to control the desire to release himself.

Dusty moved Ruth's head away from its position, pulled her towards him, putting his hands under her buttocks and moved her into position, straddling him. She could feel him slide deep inside her, and she began to rock herself back and forth finding a perfect rhythm. Her inner juices began to flow and her body started to shake uncontrollably. Dusty could contain himself no longer, and as his body stiffened, he let out a cry of pleasure as his sperm exploded inside of her. Once complete, his body vibrated as he collapsed in exhaustion. Ruth slid over his hip, curled up in the crook of his arm, and laid her arm over his limp body. They looked at each other and smiled.

"What you do to me. I have never had a woman make me feel this way," he whispered softly.

"The two of us together is incredible. It is always new, never boring, and the energy is so intense between us when we make love. It is a feeling we cannot deny."

Dusty agreed, stifled a yawn, and said, "Time for us to get some sleep, sweetheart. Tomorrow will come early, and we have a busy day ahead of us." He gently kissed her lips, and Ruth rolled over and felt the warmth of his bare backside against the small of her back. She fell asleep with a smile of pure physical satisfaction on her face.

The morning sun was just starting to peek over the horizon as the alarm on Dusty's cellphone rang, bringing the two of them out of a deep sleep. Dusty rolled over to face Ruth, "Good morning, gorgeous," he said as he sat up on the edge of the bunk.

Ruth smiled; she loved how he called her gorgeous. He could be so romantic. Ruth knew how much he loved her by the way he treated her when they were together, and how his attention increased when they were apart. She tried to understand the predicament he was in when it came to leaving Loretta. It would be hard for him to move forward without the guilt Ruth knew was keeping him from ending their relationship.

Loretta depended on Dusty for everything. Prior to their relationship, she was surviving on social assistance. She had a house that was rented, and Dusty paid the expenses. She had an eighteen-year-old son who lived at home, and whom Dusty also supported. Loretta did not work nor seemed to have any desire to work to help Dusty support the family.

She drove his new Dodge half-ton truck around the neighbourhood and transported family members to appointments and to their obligations. Dusty only went to visit. He did not even have keys to the house she lived in.

If she was not home when he arrived, there was an extra set of keys hanging inside the shed door for him to gain access. If Dusty left, Loretta would have no choice but to return to social assistance to survive or to find another man who would support her.

When Ruth and Dusty heard from dispatch about the deliveries they were to make for the day and what their schedule was going to be, they quickly grabbed coffee and headed out onto the streets of Toronto. Their day was filled with pickups and deliveries throughout the Greater Toronto Area. Dusty hated the short runs to and from the loading docks. He hated driving the 401 in traffic, and continually complained about the drivers who disregarded the size of the truck as he tried to make his way down the highway.

Ruth as a driver now recognized how annoying uneducated drivers could be when they cut off the big trucks by darting in and out in front of them. They did not seem to care about the importance of the spaces the truckers left between themselves and the vehicles ahead of them in case of sudden stops. They sped down the feeder lanes and ramps to get ahead of the trucks. They did not want to have to slow down and end up behind them.

There were many close calls between tractor trailers and passenger vehicles. Ruth had also seen semis off the road in ditches—the drivers having to ditch the truck to avoid the disaster that could have happened when the driver of the family of four cut them off in traffic at high speeds.

"I wish drivers understood how hard it is for us to stop," Dusty said in a frustrated voice. "There are too many people behind the wheels of cars who think we can stop on a dime just like them. Every driver of a vehicle should have to spend some time in the seat of a semi before getting their licence. It might give them a bit more insight and respect for what semi drivers deal with on a daily basis."

Ruth agreed. She always tried to give a semi room and would make way for them to do what they needed to do to try and navigate through traffic and on the highway. This only came from her growing up around them. She had been taught there were times the drivers of the big trucks could not see the small vehicles speeding up alongside them. The vehicle would sit in the truck's blind spot or tailgate so close they could not be seen in the rear-view mirrors. Most of the trailers now had signs, "If you can't see my mirrors, I can't see you," on the back of their trailers as warnings for drivers of passenger vehicles.

Ruth was happy to see these signs showing up more and more on the back of the trailers. It was a good way to remind passenger car drivers that the driver of the semi may not see them when they darted behind the trailer.

Ruth, as a truck driver, had more than one close call with a passenger car. It made her jerk the wheel to avoid putting the car off the road. It was a scary manoeuvre. The load could shift and the result would be an upset truck and trailer on top of the car. She tried to be more careful when changing lanes, and made sure she had more than enough room to move over.

The trip back to Sydney was uneventful. Ruth drove most of the way and was enjoying being behind the wheel.

The open road and driving were what she had always longed to do. She was getting more and more used to handling the big truck through tight construction sites, over narrow bridges, and having to deal with shifting down quickly to slow down when a flag man sign appeared. She came upon a line up because a big rig was off the road, and prayed no one had been hurt as she crawled by the scene.

Ruth was surprised at how often it came up that a semi was off the road. The drivers of the big rigs seemed to get the blame for the accidents. Little attention in the media was given to the drivers of the cars. If there was no indication of braking by the truck and trailer, it was usually always a case of the driver nodding off while driving.

The ELD system pushed drivers more than the paper logbooks of old. The ELD allowed for little sleep, and dispatch expected the drivers to drive out their allotted time of twelve-to-thirteen hours. There were cases of the paper logs causing drivers to drive harder, but with every system, there were those who liked it and those who did not.

Dusty did not like the ELD system. He believed he did not drive as hard on the paper logbooks. He could jimmy the hours to fit his driving schedule and his awake hours. In the old days, the truck was not satellite tracked. He could start and stop when he wanted and rest when he needed to. Dispatch was on his case with the ELD to drive longer and drive harder when he was exhausted from the day.

Accidents with semis had increased and were on the upswing. More and more drivers at the wheel were unfamiliar with driving in winter conditions. They paid less attention to the conditions of the road. They would drive when most seasoned drivers were parked for the night. It was all for the sake of money, profit margin, and the companies they were working for. There was no interest in the safety of the driver, the truck, or the load. Insurance premiums were climbing and starting to eat into the bottom line of all the companies.

Ruth had visited Humboldt, Saskatchewan, with the tour. She went to the site of where a semi had collided with a bus full of hockey players. It had been recorded as one of the worst motor vehicle accidents in the history of the country. The scene of the accident had resonated with Ruth. She could still feel the effect of visiting the site. Flowers, commemorations to the players, candles, stuffed animals, and pictures crowded the area.

It was because of this accident and some of the fly-by-night driver training programs that the government was looking into the practices of licensing truckers. The changes to the present system were supposed to be forthcoming. There were truck drivers out there who, for a cash payment, would teach drivers to go ahead, back up and drive down the road, with very few miles of experience. There was no real training on how the truck worked and what was expected of you once you were out on the road alone.

There were companies who were training their own drivers and testing them. This allowed for corners to be cut in training and for shorter terms of learning. There were a lot of loop holes in the driver training system. It was because of these loop holes that officials from government, trucking organizations, and companies were sitting at the table to discuss how the system could be improved. They were exploring what changes needed to be made to the present rules and regulations within the industry. The goal was to improve the overall safety, both of truckers and of drivers of passenger vehicles of all sizes, while travelling the country's highways.

Ruth knew there were major dangers out there she would have to try and avoid while driving a big rig. She paid attention to the trucks and trailers while driving her half ton across the country. Most drivers did not. She witnessed more than one close call. The other danger on the road Ruth noticed were the many people who drove recreational vehicles and hauled travel trailers. There was no training required for those who hooked up or sat behind the wheel of these huge vehicles and motored down the road. There were never-ending dangers for the truckers out there to try and keep their trucks, trailers, and loads on the road.

When the truck pulled into the R.A.E. yard, Ruth had mixed feelings about finally completing her internship. She was anxious about taking a road test with the company that would ensure her a job. She had been travelling with Dusty in the truck for over a year, and she already felt like she worked there. She knew the drivers and the administration, and developed what she thought was a good rapport.

They all knew about Dusty, Loretta, and herself, but she overlooked the strange looks she was given. She saw the looks on their faces and knew they were all the topic of water cooler conversation. She had never cared about what other people thought of what or why she did the things she did. She was always able to ignore the strange stares and comments that were made behind her back.

The guys at the shop had been digging Dusty about the relationship he shared with her. Negative comments had been made about him having two women in his life. Ruth tried to overlook all that Dusty told her. She had long since learned not to pay attention to what others said about her and how she did things. She had worked hard for what she had, always focused on what was important, and had been very lucky in receiving everything she needed when the time came. Everything in due course. The road had always met her needs, whether it be in life or in general.

Ruth learned over the years to let negative people and their opinions go. She had no clue about the entertainment industry when she started. She hardly knew anyone in the field. When she started making contacts in the field, she found those contacts would point her in the right direction to other contacts, and the event coordinator position became easier with every phone call or email.

Ruth knew the rewards of hard work. She was a workaholic, and when driven, seemed to move mountains in a positive direction that would benefit her. Dusty had a hard time believing all Ruth told him. Ruth saw how negative he could be. He was ruled by the word "can't," which Ruth had long ago eliminated from her vocabulary. Anything was possible, as far as she was concerned, with focus, hard work, and the ability to see her doing whatever it was she wanted to do in the future.

Ruth was tired of the digs and the behind-her-back chatter at R.A.E. She learned more and more while travelling with Dusty that R.A.E. was not where she wanted to work. She would find somewhere else to go that suited her needs and desires far better. Their return from this trip was no different. The boys in the shop snickered behind their backs as Ruth and Dusty climbed down from the truck. Ruth ignored them as she walked through the garage to the washroom. "Hi, guys. Sure is nice out there, eh?"

Dusty busied himself getting things done and finding out where he was to go next. Ruth went to meet up with Ricky, the man who was to take her out for her road test. Ruth liked Ricky. Her previous road test with him, when she received her Class One licence, had gone well. That test determined her skill set, and what she needed to work on driving her internship.

Ruth laughed with Ricky as they walked towards the truck. Ruth went over the pre-trip inspection and tried to back the truck up to the trailer for a coupling. She was nervous and could not seem to pull herself together. Ricky noticed how nervous she was and tried to help her calm down.

Ruth finally achieved the coupling and they pulled out of the yard. Ruth tried to shift the gears on the truck she had driven into the yard shortly before. The gears did not seem to want to work. She lost track of what gear she was in, found it hard to concentrate, and was frustrated with herself for the simple, unnecessary mistakes she was making.

"I do not know what is wrong with me. I drove the truck here all the way from Ontario."

Ricky continued to try and calm her nerves as she stalled the truck on the off ramp and tried to force the truck into gear. Ruth's frustration was starting to reflect on her driving test. It was not long before Ricky said, "Let's take it back to the yard. We are not getting very far this way."

Ruth nodded in agreement and turned the truck around and drove back to the yard. Ruth realized she was not ready to go on the road alone. She doubted herself too much. Dusty had been supportive and encouraging, but Ruth had questions in her own mind. She wondered if he was trying to get her out of the truck, more than focusing on her ability to drive.

Ricky went into the office to meet with the dispatcher and Dusty to discuss the results of the road test. Ruth knew what the outcome would be and resigned herself to the idea that working with R.A.E. was not going to pan out. She would have to start looking for a job somewhere else. Her resume was done, and she knew she had a lot to offer. She began to wonder if trucking was supposed to be her focus or was she destined for some other profession. Was it time for her to let Dusty go, and to let go of her idea and dream of owning her own truck and her own trucking fleet? Should she quit and wait for something else to come along to point her in another direction.

Once she was done at the office, she and Dusty left the yard and went to the school for her to pick up her graduation certificate. They met Terry and discussed her internship, where she was in relation to her driving skills, and what could be done to help her achieve her goal. She was a full graduate of the school now, but she did not have the ability to drive down the road alone.

After receiving her diploma and giving Terry a hug, Ruth and Dusty left his office. She had an overwhelming sense of achievement and was extremely proud of herself for all she had accomplished. She had been very nervous when she started school, and, as she walked towards the exit, she was a bit sad it was over. She had completed her course and would not be returning. She stepped out of the building into a bright new future.

CHAPTER 6
Dealing with Setbacks

Ruth and Dusty went back to the yard, and Dusty showered her with praises about her completing the course. He told her how proud he was of her and not to worry about messing up the road test. "You will get it next time. Dispatch offered you another trip to practice, and then when you return, you can take another test. If you pass, you're in. If not, then they will let you go," he said.

Ruth was grateful for the additional opportunity to go away with Dusty and take the second road test. She was not sure, after all she had learned about R.A.E., the way the company was run and some of the employees, whether she really wanted to work there. She started to lean towards looking for work elsewhere. She had grown tired of the ups and downs that Dusty's relationship with Loretta presented. She questioned her own involvement in the tricky triangle that had developed between the three of them. It was not healthy for any of them, yet, she still could not figure out what made her gravitate to him.

She had tried to walk away from the relationship. She had threatened to quit during her internship, had threatened all kinds of things. She could not find it within herself to carry out the threats. She had never met anyone she could not seem to do without or walk away from. There had been many men in her life over the years. Some she thought, at one point or another, could have been a potential partner.

She had lived inside a relationship with her ex-husband where there always seemed to be other women. She had eventually left him, but for some reason she was finding it difficult to walk away from Dusty and the promises he made to her about a future life together. She thought the fire that burned between them may dwindle out over the months, but as they continued to unite it appeared the fire was getting stronger with every union.

She knew the possibilities were there for him and her to have a relationship. They had such fun together. She could not figure out what he was afraid of when it seemed to come time for him to leave Loretta. He had gone to the house, spent a couple of days, and left. Loretta did her thing, he did his. When he returned to the mainland, Ruth knew where he had been and welcomed him back with open arms.

They continued their relationship as if he had never been with another woman. There was no question in her mind that Dusty loved her. She could not figure out why he refused to leave. Most of the time, Ruth was able to put the relationship between Dusty and Loretta out of her mind. Other times, it drove her crazy—especially when Dusty would call and complain about Loretta and the big fights that erupted between the two of them.

Once Ruth and Dusty arrived at the yard, Ruth put the pickup in park and turned towards Dusty. "I am going to the barn to see Waylon. It has been a long day, and I could use the ride. Do you want me to come back and pick you up or are you going to meet me at home?"

"I have a few things to finish up here. I will meet you at home. Enjoy your ride," he said opening the door and stepping out.

Ruth knew Dusty would take the time to call Loretta. He could do it without worry of Ruth interrupting the conversation and of Loretta not finding out he was with Ruth. He would finish his conversation and then drive over to meet her at their apartment.

Ruth pulled out of the R.A.E. yard and headed down the road towards the barn. She had been away for over a week and was looking forward to seeing Waylon and taking a ride. She still had a hard time believing she had been able to purchase him.

Waylon was green when she brought him to Sydney and had forgotten most of the training she had put him through the previous summer. Now he was visibly happy to see her when she returned. She entered the barn and called his name. He lifted his head and whinnied. They had started to bond again. She grabbed her saddle, blanket, and bridle from the tack room and walked towards his stall.

Ruth climbed up into the saddle and a sense of calm came over her. She steered Waylon out into the field. She directed him towards the trail and they started through the woods. The trail led to a lake, and it was a nice ride through the trees. She could smell the forest, and enjoyed the peace and quiet of riding. It had been quite a while since she had been on his back, and she welcomed the feeling of being back in the saddle.

As she came around a turn in the trail, a white-tailed deer bounced out of the woods. Its sudden appearance startled both her and Waylon. Ruth grabbed the horn of the saddle as Waylon bolted down the trail. She pulled on the reins to slow him down, and he stopped short. His sudden movement caught her off balance. Ruth lost her seat and landed hard on the ground, hitting her head.

Ruth tried to get up after the sudden fall. Her head was spinning, and she could not seem to get her footing. Her stomach started to feel queasy as she tried to stand. Waylon stood still, looking at her, and then slowly started toward her. She grabbed the reins and pulled him closer to her, then used the stirrup to steady herself while she attempted to stand. She stood there for a few minutes to give herself time to let the dizziness pass. She urged Waylon ahead slowly and held onto the saddle as she stumbled along beside him until her head cleared.

She knew something was seriously wrong, and she was not going to be able to walk the distance back to the barn. Ruth stopped Waylon, straightened the stirrup enough to put her foot in, and pulled herself back up onto the saddle. Waylon started ahead once she was seated and slowly made his way down the trail. Ruth let the reins lay limp against his neck and held herself in place by hanging onto the saddle horn.

Her head felt clearer when she got back to the barn, and she slowly stripped his tack and returned it to the tack room. She gave Waylon his carrot and apple and then made her way to her pickup to call Dusty.

"Hi, Dusty. I just took a nasty fall off Waylon and I am going to go to the emergency room to get checked out," she said trying to sound like she wasn't worried.

"Are you sure you can drive, Ruth? I can come get you if you want," Dusty replied, sounding concerned.

"No, I am sure, I will be fine. I will call you once I am on my way home," Ruth said

"Okay, keep me posted. I will come to the hospital to get you if they won't let you drive."

Ruth drove herself to the emergency department and went through triage. She patiently waited to be seen by a doctor. She had never liked hospitals and was not a very good patient. She was starting to feel better as she sat waiting. The doctor arrived and asked her a lot of questions. The diagnosis was she had a concussion. "You should not be alone for the next forty-eight hours. Get lots of rest and relaxation for the next couple of days. If you are still not coming around, come back." Ruth thanked the doctor, called Dusty to tell him she was on her way home, and slowly walked out of the hospital and to her truck.

That night, Ruth and Dusty sat and watched television. She dozed, off and on, and then crawled into bed. Dusty put his arm around her and she snuggled up to him, instantly falling asleep.

The next few weeks were uneventful for Ruth. She was unable to drive and a CT scan showed a subdural hematoma. Ruth went over the scan results with the doctor. It was going to be quite some time before she was able to drive again. He scheduled her for a second scan and then they would review the results again to determine when she could resume her position behind the wheel.

"No riding, no driving a rig, until we see the results of the second scan. I cannot let you go down the road without knowing for sure you are fit to be behind the wheel," the doctor said.

Ruth was disappointed and, despite the fall, she was anxious to get back in the saddle and behind the wheel. She came home, called Dusty, and told him about her doctor's visit. "Well, everything else is not very important. You need to get well. You will be back behind the wheel and in the saddle before you know it."

"I know," she replied half-heartedly, "I know."

The days rolled into each other and Dusty stayed in touch by telephone. Ruth began to think about her future and where it might lead. It would be after Thanksgiving before she would be able to get behind the wheel again. She would be facing winter without having driven a mile for two months.

It would be like starting all over again. Her shifting would deteriorate while she was off, and what she had learned would start to fade. She started thinking she might go back to school and do something different. She did not like the thought of not travelling with Dusty.

Abby was due home from England for a visit before Thanksgiving. Ruth was looking forward to seeing her and catching up on all the news. Abby would certainly have her say on what she thought about Ruth, the accident, and her trucking career. Ruth was ready for it. Abby had to clear the air and tell Ruth what she thought. Sometimes, it annoyed Ruth, but she was getting used to it.

Ruth said little to Abby when she started spouting off, and she let Abby's comments roll off her shoulders. Ruth agreed, thanked Abby for her input, and then let it slide. They only saw each other once a year. Ruth did not want to upset the apple cart while she was visiting. Ruth had been trying for years to reach Abby, without success. Ruth was determined to not make waves and to enjoy Abby's company.

Ruth and Ambrose had chatted, off and on, since she had moved to Sydney. Ambrose was working full time as an electrician and was starting to earn a good salary. His girlfriend was still in school and would be graduating in the spring. Ruth was happy that Ambrose was out on his own and was hoping her ex-husband would soon consider putting the house up for sale.

The house held twenty years of stuff, to which Ruth had no attachment. There were only a few things that belonged to her mother and father, and a few items that held sentimental value, that she would keep. She would have no problem packing up her few remaining belongings and putting them in storage when the time came. Abby had some things there, too. Ruth planned to discuss with Abby sharing a storage unit, where they could lock away the items that meant the most to them.

It would be too expensive for Abby to ship all her childhood memories to England, so a storage unit was the best option for both of them. Ambrose had some of his belongings in the house, too. He could store them in the unit, until such a time he made the decision on what he wanted to do with it all.

Ruth sat in her living room staring out the window and having her morning coffee. It was raining and she would be staying inside again trying to decide the best way to spend her time. She started to apply for trucking jobs online, and then she would go to the barn and do liberty training with Waylon. He was catching on quickly, and they had fun playing together in the arena. She did not watch a lot of television, so her evenings were long. She spent a lot of time staring into space, mulling over in her mind what she wanted to do if trucking did not work out.

Ruth remembered the previous year she had been so frustrated with the tour and was wondering what to do. Trucking had come along and put Ruth on a path she never dreamed would happen. But, once again, here she sat, wondering if trucking was the route she wanted to go. Now, after the riding accident, she began to wonder would she ever be able to drive a semi again.

CHAPTER 7

New Beginnings

Ruth's train of thought was interrupted by the ringing of her cellphone. She saw it was Ambrose and was surprised he would be calling her in the middle of the day. Ruth got an uneasy feeling as she picked it up and said, "Hello."

"Mom, I have some bad news. You need to come home right away," Ambrose said with a tremble in his voice.

"What is it, Ambrose? I can leave now. It won't take me long to get there. What's going on?"

"It's Dad. He was at the gym. They had to call an ambulance. They are rushing him to the hospital. It doesn't look good. I'm on my way there now. You need to come home."

Ruth told Ambrose to keep her posted on his father's condition and assured him she would be on the road within the hour. It was a six-hour drive and she would be there as soon as she could.

Ruth gathered her things and threw them in a bag. She pulled her jacket off the hanger on her way out the door, closed and locked it behind her as she ran out to her Chevy.

Ruth drove out of the driveway of her apartment building and turned out onto the highway. As she drove, a million things went through her mind. She and her ex-husband had remained friends after the separation. He lived a lonely life and was pretty much a recluse. He had a few friends he went to the gym with, on a regular basis, to walk and get some exercise. He would stop on his way home at Tim Hortons, where he sat and chatted with friends before making his way back to the house.

He was ex-military, and, after his return from overseas, had never been the same. Ruth tried her best to keep things running smoothly between them, but it had not been an easy job. His illnesses overtook him, and there was no way to break down the internal walls he had built around himself. Ruth had to finally admit defeat and carry on with her life.

It had been hard on all of them. Abby and Ambrose were young when their father had first taken ill. There were days Ruth did not know whether she could continue or not. It was the children who kept her going. Ruth's own health had started to suffer. Her doctor advised her if she didn't start taking care of herself, there would be no one to take care of anyone else.

Ruth listened and had taken the necessary steps to begin the process of freeing herself from the life she was deteriorating in. She had gone to visit an old school friend in Calgary. A relationship was born, and it began the process of Ruth beginning to realize she had her own life to live. She started flying back and forth between Alberta and Nova Scotia, trying to juggle both worlds. It worked for a while, but eventually their relationship had come to an end.

That was when she became involved with the tour. She met many professional entertainers in Calgary and had taken to the industry like a moth to a flame. She loved it in the beginning, but as time went on, she became disillusioned with the industry. When she met Dusty that morning at breakfast, she found trucking was to be the next step in her journey.

Dusty was still involved with Loretta, and Ruth was beginning to think he would never leave. Loretta stalked Ruth on social media, and Ruth was beginning to resent the whole situation. Dusty refused to make a decision, so Ruth walked away from the relationship. She was tired of waiting and was ready to move on with her life. So, one night on the phone, she told him not to contact her again until he had decided to move out and away from Loretta.

Ambrose called and updated her. It was not looking good, and Ruth assured him she was driving as fast as she could without being dangerous to herself and others. People always teased her about having a lead foot. As she now held a Class One licence, she was more aware of her speed and had slowed down considerably when driving. The last thing she needed was a speeding ticket on her new licence. She had found it hard to get a job right out of school, and the concussion had set her back. A speeding ticket would only add a black mark on her driving abstract and set her back that much further.

Ruth thought about how this, too, could set her back even further. If her ex-husband didn't make it, there would be lots of work to do at the house to get it ready to sell. It could take weeks to pack it up, and to settle his estate and matters that should have been dealt with a long time ago. Ruth had more than once tried to encourage him to let the place go and move into a self-contained apartment, but he refused to move. Ruth agreed to wait until he was ready, before liquidating the last of their assets.

Ruth pulled up and parked in the hospital parking lot. She grabbed her purse and started towards the door. Ambrose was waiting in the lobby. "I tried to call you, but you must have been in a place with no service. Dad passed away about a half hour ago. I figured when I did not get you on the phone, I would wait until you got here."

Ruth felt tears welling up in her eyes, but she could not cry. She could see Ambrose had been crying, but he stood strong before her. Ambrose wrapped his arms around her and they held each other for a few minutes. Ruth stepped back and said quietly, "Have you called Abby?"

"No, she is still at work in England. I could call Caleb and tell him, but I thought it might be good to wait until we knew what was going on first."

"Good idea. Let's go and find out where we go from here."

Ruth and Ambrose sat down with the doctor and went over the accident and what had transpired up until then.

"We did everything we could. He had a heart attack in the shower, fell, and cracked his head on the side of the shower wall. He was attended to immediately. There was nothing anyone could do. I am so sorry for your loss," the doctor said quietly.

Ruth nodded. She had been through this before when her parents passed away. Her sister had been with her for support. Now, she was the mother and did not want to lean on Ambrose. It was going to be hard for Abby. She was not looking forward to the call. At least, Abby had been home recently and had been able to spend some time with her father alone.

It wasn't long before the hospital staff were asking what they wanted to do, and Ruth went into organizational mode. She contacted the funeral home, made the cremation arrangements, and then she and Ambrose went back to the house to call Abby. It was coming on to winter, and Abby had just started a new job. She had been home for Thanksgiving, and having to leave England again to come back to Canada for a funeral was not something Ruth wanted to tell her. There would be lots to be done and Abby would not be able to stay. Ruth and Ambrose decided the best course of action would be to hold off on the funeral until next year, when Abby returned with Caleb for their summer vacation. The family could have a quiet, simple, private graveside service.

Ruth would be able to get things organized, and the house packed up and on the market. Maybe by the time Abby returned the house would be sold. Ruth did not want to come back and move in for the winter months.

The memories in the house were too hard to even think about. She had visited and stayed there from time to time when there was business to discuss, but now, it was only a house. She welcomed it gone. She knew it would be hard for Abby. Ambrose had moved on and was living on his own with Samantha. Abby moved to England almost a decade ago, but she still felt like it was home for her. Abby was going to take the news hard.

Ruth picked up the phone and dialed the number. It was nine o'clock in the evening in England. She was hoping Caleb was home to give her the support she was going to need.

"Hi, Mom. How are you?" Abby's voice filtered through the phone.

"Hey, Abby. I'm okay. How are you? How was your day? How is the new job going?"

"It is going great. I love it. I like what I am doing and the people I work with. I have a lot to learn, but that will come."

"Is Caleb home?"

"Yes, he is sitting right here. We are watching television."

"Abby, I have some bad news," Ruth began slowly as she tried to choose her words carefully, "Your father passed away this morning. I waited to call until you were home from work. I wanted Caleb to be home with you when you got the news."

There was a silence on the phone, and then Ruth heard Abby burst into tears. Caleb's voice came over the phone, "We will book a flight home immediately. We should be there in the morning."

"Wait, Caleb. We are not going ahead with any funeral arrangements right now. With winter coming on and Abby just starting a new job, Ambrose and I have been talking, and we will wait until the two of you come home next summer. Abby was just home, and there is a lot to be done here at the house. Do not book your flights right now. Hold off and I will keep you posted as things unfold over here."

"Okay, I will try and explain that to Abby, but right now, it will not be easy."

Ruth knew Abby was going to have a hard time with her father's death. Ruth and Caleb chatted a bit longer as Ruth passed on the details of the accident and what her plans were. Ruth would call again when things were a bit more settled.

Ambrose looked at his Mother and put his arm around her, "Are you okay?"

"Yes, it was a hard phone call to make. I knew it would be before I dialed the number. I'm glad it's over," Ruth sighed into his shoulder.

Ambrose stepped back and said, "I'm going to fix myself a drink. Do you want one?"

"Absolutely, I think after today we could both use one," Ruth said with a smile.

Ruth and Ambrose sat and chatted over their drinks about the past, present, and future. They discussed the selling of the house and packing up its contents. There were so many memories, good and bad, and they chuckled at the funny events. The memories of the kids, past holidays, and they both felt the loss of something in their own way.

"Do you want me to stay the night? I will give Samantha a call. She will understand."

"No, you go home. I will be fine here alone. I have some things I want to do."

Ruth stood on the veranda and watched Ambrose pull out of the driveway. It was one of her favourite spots to sit when she was at the house. The veranda was covered and allowed her the solace and comfort of sitting with a beverage, no matter what the weather.

Ruth picked up the house phone and started to listen to the many messages that had been left by her ex-husband's friends. She returned their phone calls first, then dialed his nephew to pass on the news to the rest of his family. She had not spoken to any of them in years.

They did not understand his post-traumatic stress disorder or any of his other illnesses and had withdrawn from him. He was not the man they grew up with or knew any longer. So, instead of making an effort to keep in touch, they had gone on with their lives without him being included.

It troubled her ex-husband the way people had broken away from him, and he had no idea how to repair the damage that had been done over the years. He continued to live in his own little world, without letting anyone else in. He had grown cold and distant, and people felt it.

Ruth had been sad for the loss of her ex-husband to the disorder. While seeking help for herself, she realized there was absolutely nothing she could do for him, so she had given up and moved on with her life. He and she had grown so far apart they both knew there was no way to repair the damage done to their marriage.

Once her phone calls were made, she started sorting through papers and documents. She would need to go to the bank, settle matters there, contact insurance companies, lawyers, and have his will read. Ruth looked at the clock; it was almost midnight. She stopped her work, made a cup of tea, and returned to the veranda. She reflected on the forty-plus years she had been with her ex-husband and smiled at the good memories.

They had been high school sweethearts and had big dreams back then. He decided to join the Canadian Armed Forces. That was the beginning of the end. He was away so much. Ruth was an extremely independent woman. She had grown up in a family of five, and Ruth's parents were older when she was born.

This left her without a mother and father very early in life. While growing up, they prepared her to make her own decisions. They left her to run wild and live her life the way she saw fit. Ruth spent a lot of time on her own during her teen years. When her ex-husband came into her life, she had little room in her life for a partner.

After six years of dating, they married. Ruth knew now, it had been a mistake. She stayed with him over the years for security, and then when the children came, she dedicated herself to raising them. He was away from home a lot. She spent most of her time concentrating on Abby and Ambrose. He had tried to join their small family circle when he returned from away, but there never seemed to be room for him. He was only home for short periods of time, then he was gone again.

When he became ill, it was a nightmare for Ruth. There had been so much uncertainty with regard to their future. They moved, and there were questions regarding their financial future and security. The children were small, and times were tough. There were doctor's appointments, tests, and hospital stays, while a medical team tried to figure out what was happening to him.

He became distant, locked himself away from everyone, and she could not figure out why. Everything seemed to be her fault. He slowly became more distant and colder towards her and everyone around him. The children were busy with school activities. They barely noticed what was happening around them.

Abby was almost five years older than Ambrose. She remembered some of the hard times. There was a Christmas without presents, strangers showing up at their door with food, times when they had little, but Ruth had managed to keep things going one way or the other.

Ruth's health suffered through those years. She gained weight, she was depressed, she was like a robot. She got up every morning and went about her day without any feeling whatsoever. She supported her children in whatever they did. Ambrose played rugby; Abby played basketball. They were involved in school clubs and did well academically.

It was a bittersweet feeling for Ruth as she sat looking out over the landscape in front of the veranda. There had been so many times she had to come back here, but did not want to. She had come only because of the children. The house was big enough for all of them, and it was a gathering place whenever Abby came home.

Ruth was comfortable in her little apartment in Sydney, but now that she had accepted a job with Nationwide Transport, it would no longer be necessary for her to keep it. It was Ruth's intention to move completely into and live out of her truck.

The decision had not come easily. Dusty and she had had such a great relationship. They had fun together, and she felt she could tell him anything. The situation had gone on far too long, and Ruth was tired of it. She had written him a few weeks before to tell him she did not want to continue. He agreed to respect her decision. He advised her if she ever needed him, she knew how to get in touch. She had done the same. Ruth knew it left the door open for both of them. It was a phone call that probably would not be made. Ruth knew, as soon as she was going down the road in her own truck and stopping at truck stops along the way, the possibility of running into him would become greater. She would cross that bridge when she came to it.

She thought about calling him to let him know about the demise of her ex-husband, but decided against it. She had too much to do over the next few weeks to open that door again, and she had much to think about over the coming months.

Ruth finished her tea and walked into the house. She went into her bedroom and shut the door. There was so much going through her mind. She crawled into bed and turned out the light. She was saddened by the death of her ex-husband, but realized it was truly the beginning of a new life for her.

CHAPTER 8

Starting Over

The next few weeks were a flurry of activity for Ruth. She had so much to do and to settle before getting back to her job. She closed up the house for the winter and walked away, leaving it for another day. She remembered her mother doing the same thing when her father passed away.

It was easy for her to leave the house. She was not ready to deal with everything that needed to be done. The cleaning and packing would have to wait until Abby returned from England the following summer. Ambrose promised to keep an eye on the place for the winter, and Ruth trusted him to do so. It was just a house to him, too. He would visit, from time to time, to make sure the pipes did not freeze and that everything was as they had left it.

Ruth was not sure what she was going to do with it all. She would probably do the same as her mother. She would call someone in the spring to come and arrange an open house yard sale, maybe an auction. She would rent a storage unit to store the heirlooms she had kept from her parents and the stuff that was most important to her. Abby could utilize the storage unit for the things that were too expensive to ship. Ambrose had a place of his own. What he would do with his things when the time came would be up to him.

Ruth went back on the road. She was grateful for the solace of the truck. She was giving serious thought to owning her own truck. She mentally monitored the truck she drove and was keeping notes on expenses. She dreamed of owning and then forming a company and having a small fleet.

The nights and days blended as Ruth travelled down the road making drops and pickups. The weather did not keep her from driving. She never felt unsafe in her truck, no matter what the road conditions. She worked hard, turned around when asked, and never complained about her job. She liked working for Nationwide Transport. Ruth was sure that being in her own truck was helping her adjust to being on her own and alone again. She encountered many other truckers, married and single, but paid little attention to them.

When she arrived in truck stops for the night, she parked her truck, went inside to shower, and returned to her truck. She ate in her truck, kept to herself, and curled up every night alone in her bunk. Her last relationship was with Dusty, and she was not interested in dating. Men tried to talk to her. She was polite and went about her business. She put up an internal wall that no one, no matter how nice, could break down.

Her only focus was to drive, get to her destination, and drive again. She came home to Sydney to the peace and quiet of her little apartment, spent her home time with Waylon, and then went out on the road again.

She would see quite a few of the truckers she had met when she was travelling with Dusty. She nodded or acknowledged them, but she did not stop to talk. She did not want Dusty knowing who she was driving for or where she was. She disappeared from his life as rapidly as she had come into it that morning in Aulac. She knew he was out there, and every time she saw the R.A.E. trucks on the road, her heart skipped a beat.

She did not purposely avoid the truck stops she knew he visited. He was a creature of habit, and she knew the day would come when they would see each other again somewhere.

Some of the truckers contacted her to see if she was okay and where she was. She knew they were calling to try and obtain information on her whereabouts for Dusty. Nathan continued to contact her and keep in touch. She was careful not to tell him who she was driving for or where she was. She knew he would relay the information back to Dusty. Vernon was in touch once or twice. She had great respect for him, and it was good to hear from him. She let him know she was doing fine and on the road.

She avoided the other company drivers, including Byron, George, Thomas, and those she knew when she saw them in the truck stops. She was distant, and they did not approach her. She would refuel, get coffee, and be on her way.

Ruth returned to the West many times, and one night she found herself in Regina sitting in the truck stop where she first met Doris so long ago. Doris was happy to see her. They sat together having coffee while getting caught up on all the news of the truckers she knew.

Ruth was shocked and saddened to learn that Gabe had died in a fiery crash, and Mad Maxx was no longer on the road. Ruth reflected on their meeting when she returned to the truck. So many truckers lost their lives in one way or another. Ruth knew Gabe had died the way he would have wanted to, in the seat of his truck. It was a good end to the life of a dedicated trucker.

The more miles she could log, the better. She was turning out to be one of their best employees, the one they depended on to get the job done. She was willing to do whatever they asked and did not once complain or argue when they asked her to turn around.

She spent her spare time on resets in her truck. She welcomed the time to relax and be lazy. The reset days made her cherish the days she did not have to get up and jump into the driver's seat. She would make herself a cup of coffee and hardly ever poked her nose beyond the curtains. The most time she spent in truck stops was to do her laundry and shower. Once the things in the truck stop were done, she retreated back to her truck until it was time to roll out of the truck stop and go.

She watched the sun rise and fall over so many provinces and states, she barely knew where she was most times. She lost track of the days. Pickup and delivery days were the only things that reminded her what day it was. She often checked her calendar to determine the exact date, and if she was on time. She rarely ran behind schedule. She was dependable and did her best to make sure she was either early or right on time, unless weather or traffic delayed her.

That was one thing she had learned from Dusty. Be on time, do your best, and get to know the customers—they would help you, if you helped them. Be nice, polite, and not one of the drivers who complained all the time. Dusty had a love-hate relationship with his dispatcher. Ruth was the opposite at Nationwide. They had given her a chance, and she was going to do her best so they did not regret that decision.

Ruth spent Christmas and New Year's on the road. While she was parked, she picked up a little Christmas tree for her truck and decorated it on Christmas Eve. She spent New Year's Eve in the privacy of her truck and wondered what the new year would bring. There had been so many changes in her life over the past year. She reflected on the things she had gained and the love she had lost, and went to sleep that night with a quiet wish, *Happy New Year, Dusty.*

It was in the late days of March that she pulled into the truck stop at Aulac. It was the place where she had first met Dusty. She had been on the road by herself for almost six months and was becoming more confident with every mile. She loved to drive, she loved the job, and she was always happy to go and do whatever Nationwide asked of her.

Ruth backed her truck into a spot and smiled at how her skill at backing up was improving. She was pleased with herself. It had not been easy learning how to tuck the truck in between two others. She also knew that without practice, she would never have been able to achieve the skill. She was getting better, and she was proud of herself.

She pulled the air brakes, stood up, and closed the curtains. She was looking forward to having a shower, getting some food, and then a good night's sleep. She packed her backpack for the shower, opened her door, and stepped down onto the ground. The night was cool, crisp, and clear. She stopped to let a tractor trailer drive through before starting to walk across the parking lot to the professional drivers' door.

She stopped suddenly in the middle of the parking lot. She could not believe her eyes when she saw a man walk out from around the front end of a grey Freightliner. She did not know whether to go forward or retreat back to her truck. There was no mistaking who he was. Her heart felt like it was in her throat, and she froze.

Then, as if pushed forward, she yelled, "Dusty!" and started to run towards him. He stopped in his tracks and dropped the backpack slung over his shoulder. She leaped into his arms, and the familiar feeling of his hug surrounded her. They both started to cry as they held each other. Their kiss was as passionate as it had ever been, and she could feel his love for her had not died. Ruth knew he would be the only true love she would ever have.

Their embrace lasted a few minutes, then he stood her back down on the ground. Looking into her eyes, he said, "I cannot believe I have found you! I have been searching for you at every truck stop I have parked in. I have watched every truck that came in, hoping one of them would have you in it. I heard through Nathan you were driving, and as soon as I knew that, I started looking for you. You just disappeared. I have been searching for you ever since."

Ruth looked at him and smiled, "I too, have been watching for you at every truck stop, hoping I would see you again someday, and trying not to lose faith that I would."

Dusty took her hand and led her towards his truck. "Let me drop my backpack, and let's go sit somewhere and catch up."

Ruth followed. "I was going to get something to eat, then take a shower. I am waiting on a pickup in Moncton, but ran out of time, so I am here for the night. What is your schedule like?"

"I am here for the night, too, on my way back to the yard. I just pulled in. I was going to take a shower, but that can wait. I would much rather spend time with you."

They settled into a booth and ordered dinner. The waitresses teased them about being there together again. They knew their story and had continued to watch for when the two of them would be reunited. Ruth could not stop looking at him, as if, by some twist of fate, he would disappear right before her eyes. She still felt like she was dreaming. The strength of their love was bringing them back together in the same spot in which they had first met.

Their dinner arrived and they talked, laughed, and ate. Ruth told Dusty about becoming a widow, the work that needed to be done at the house, and that she had started driving for Nationwide Transport shortly after they had broken up. Dusty told her Loretta was never able to get over their relationship, and shortly after the New Year, he had moved out and back to his mother's.

His mother and brother were well and had often asked him if he had ever seen her or heard what had happened to her. He once asked his mother to contact Ruth, but she refused and told him to call her himself. "I was afraid to. I did not know how you would react to a phone call from me."

Ruth inquired about the other drivers and how they were. Dusty was still working at R.A.E. and shook his head. "Even though they are not great to work for, they have been good to me in many ways, so I stay. I have been there eight-and-a-half years. One company is as good as the other."

Ruth told him about being on the road for Nationwide Transport and how much she enjoyed her job. "I owe it all to you, you know. It was you who got me started. I knew our paths would cross again—I just did not know when. I decided to leave it up to the universe; I knew the right time would come. I had to have faith and believe it would happen. I did not know when or where, but I knew in my heart it would."

Time passed without either one of them realizing how long they had been sitting there. The girls in the restaurant were cleaning up and advised them both it was closing time. They laughed and apologized for having been there so long.

As they got up from the table, Dusty said, "I am going to go and get my backpack to take a shower. Wanna join me?" He had a twinkle in his eye.

Ruth laughed. "I have my stuff with me. I will wait for you in the drivers' lounge."

Dusty left the restaurant while Ruth went to sit in the drivers' lounge to wait. When he returned, they registered for a shower, took the shower key, and opened the door. As they started to undress, the feelings of familiarity rushed up in Ruth. She started to undress, and Dusty reached back in the old familiar way to unclasp her bra.

They washed each other lovingly and gently, enjoying the curves of each other's body. It had been so long since she had enjoyed the pleasure of his touch. Her body had ached so many nights, and her memories had sustained her until this very moment. There was no doubt in her mind that she loved him, and she could feel from the way he caressed her body that he loved her, too.

They could not keep their eyes off one another, and their hands wandered to all the old familiar places. Passion was building between them during the shower, and they could not wait to get back to the truck to continue their reunion. As they exited the truck stop building, Ruth took Dusty's hand and steered him towards her truck.

Dusty followed her. She opened the passenger door for him to get in, and went around to the driver's door to let herself in and pulled herself up. Dusty looked around the inside of the year-old Western Star and noticed the pictures and things she had hanging from the passenger seat sun visor: the picture of his father, her father, the angel wings, how her stuffed toys sat in the spots they had in his truck. The little truck and trailer that Bob had given her graced the corner of the passenger's side of the windshield, on the dash. The rest of her truck was simple. Her coffee pot sat on the floor, and the slow cooker was tucked into the corner of the upper bunk. "It almost looks like the inside of mine," he laughed.

"I had a decorating idea, but it did not seem to fit. So, I decorated it the only way I knew, and I took the ideas from yours. It was familiar and comforting. Want a beer?" Ruth asked opening the little fridge.

"Sure," Dusty said, and took the Keith's she handed him.

Dusty popped the tops on both their drinks, and they sat and chatted. Ruth told him about her first winter on the road. "It was horrendous. There were some white-knuckle days for me. I am not sure if I want to go through that again. I am thinking about taking this winter off and only driving through the summer months from now on. I can tell you from refuelling, and working around the vans and trailers, a beach down south is looking pretty damn good right now."

"Winter driving can be tricky, depending on what you are hauling. The snow, ice, and winds can be brutal and blow you around like a kite if you do not keep a tight grip on the wheel. How are Abby and Ambrose?"

"They are both good and getting used to their mother being on the road. They have been cheering me on since I started. Abby is worried about me all the time, but she is adjusting. Ambrose is doing well and living the life of a thirty-year-old."

As they finished their beer, both of them looked at each other. Ruth had so many questions running through her head, but her body was screaming for his touch. She pushed her questions to the back of her mind.

"Do you want another beer?"

"No, this one is enough, thanks."

He stood up to put the empty bottles in the garbage and took her hand, standing her up in front of him.

"I have missed you so much," he whispered as he drew her into him and kissed her.

Before she knew it, his hands were removing her clothing and moving her towards the bunk. She pulled his T-shirt over his head and sat down on the bunk to unbuckle his belt and to move his pants down over his hips to the floor. He stood in front of her; she took his cock into her mouth and lovingly caressed it with her tongue. He responded in deep moans, and as his manhood began to grow, Ruth could feel the head reaching the back of her throat. She began moving her head back and forth slowly and rhythmically until he was rock hard. He slowly sat down beside her, lifting her legs, and moving her back on the bunk.

Ruth lay back as he lay down beside her and began caressing her nipples and running his hands over her body. Ruth moaned with pleasure as she relished the familiar feeling of the man who knew her every curve. He opened her legs and positioned himself between them. He took her buttocks in his hands and lifted her womanhood to his mouth. His hot tongue between her legs made Ruth quiver with delight. It had been so long since a man had touched her, and her body reacted immediately to his caress.

Their lovemaking was slow, easy, and intense—just as it had always been. They were both spent with pleasure, and Ruth curled up in her spot next to him with her hand on his chest. They lay there together talking and enjoying the aftermath of their reunion.

Ruth could tell by the way he reacted to her that he had missed her and still loved her—just as he always had. What they had shared together in the past, time could not erase. Their chance meeting in the truck stop had renewed a flame neither of them could deny. Ruth had known, from the very beginning, that Dusty was the man for her and had fallen head over heels in love with him when they had travelled to Regina together.

Dusty had been the same with her until Ruth found out about Loretta. The revelation made their relationship rocky. Dusty was indecisive about what he wanted, and had continually bounced between Ruth and Loretta. Ruth had gotten tired of the games and had finally made the decision to move on and disappear. It had not been easy in the beginning; she spent many nights curled up on her couch watching mindless television and really not caring what happened or went on around her. Eventually, as time went on, she got back to living and doing what she had always wanted to do.

Ruth spent her days on the road trying to move forward in her life. She had taken herself out of the game of love and was fully focused on her career. She was like a robot—with no feelings, going until she dropped, then getting up, and off she went again. Nationwide Transport was happy with her performance.

She was the type of truck driver they wanted: no questions asked, turn on a dime, and get the freight to its destination as soon as possible. They did not know how she kept the schedule she did. She was up, on the road, and going all the time. If it were not for the ELD, they would never have known where she was or what she was doing. She clocked in, made her stops, took her necessary breaks, and clocked out after her hours were spent.

Ruth and Dusty slept in each other's arms all night in the bunk of Ruth's Western Star. Her alarm was set for early morning, and she nudged him when it rang. "I have got to get going. I have a pickup to make and then have to be back on the road." Dusty knew the importance of the trucking schedule, and yet he moved towards her.

"Can you start a bit late?" he replied as he shifted position to face her.

"I suppose, just this once," Ruth smiled back and rolled into him.

They made love, got up, dressed, and went inside. They each grabbed a cup of coffee before splitting up to go to their respective trucks.

"Stay in touch today. Hopefully our schedules will come together again soon."

"I will, and you too. Drive safe."

They both climbed into their rigs and followed each other out of the parking lot. Ruth had so much going through her mind about their chance meeting, their lovemaking, and how it made her feel. She was trying to get a handle on all the old feelings that were being reignited. There was so much water under the bridge.

She tried to concentrate on what was going on around her on the highway and was happy when she reached her destination. Ruth backed into the loading dock and pulled the air brakes. It would be a couple of hours before she was loaded. She stretched out in her bunk and tried to get a handle on all the mixed feelings surrounding her reunion with Dusty the night before.

Dusty called a couple of times throughout the day. She did take one call when she was stopped. Ruth never talked on the telephone while she was driving. She put her truck in gear and went on her way down the road. She returned messages to dispatch when she stopped and was careful to make sure she checked in with her sister and Ambrose daily. Ruth usually called Abby when she was on reset or had a few hours, if the time difference did not get in the way.

The summer months rolled by as Ruth and Dusty met from time to time in truck stops along their routes. They had picked up almost where they had left off. The phone calls, text messages, and meetings were hot and full of connotations. They both worked long hours and ended each day in their individual bunks wherever they were with a phone call. Sometimes, Ruth stopped before Dusty, and vice versa, but they always seemed to be able to connect before their days were done.

They discussed buying or leasing their own truck and running team. Ruth had only been on the road a little over a year. Dusty was well established with the company he was with. He was not always happy with how they treated him, but he had benefits and so he stayed and went about his job. They both dreamed of working for themselves one day.

Dusty had almost had his own truck at one point in his life. The divorce he went through years before had taken that dream from him. Ruth had always dreamed of having her own truck and living in it on the road. Her own tiny house on wheels.

Now, it seemed to be possible. The passing of her ex-husband had given her a healthy little nest egg to work with. She was ready to take the next step in her trucking career. She wanted her own company, a small fleet, maybe six to ten trucks on the road. It was a big dream, but an obtainable dream.

They had friends who were married and team driving. Ruth envied their relationship and their lifestyle. It was what she wanted—a man who understood her love for the road, and who would be devoted to her. Charlie and Gwen were the picture of what she wanted. They were each other's best friend. Gwen had started to travel with Charlie when their children were grown. She was in the process of getting her licence and they were moving towards team driving. They leased a truck from a company in Ontario and were working together on their dream. Ruth was hoping Dusty might be ready to do the same.

One night as they lay curled in the bunk of Dusty's Freightliner, Ruth decided to start the conversation. "What do you think about us leasing with the same company Charlie and Gwen are leasing with?" she asked twisting on her side and propping herself up on her elbow to look at him.

"I am not sure. I don't know all the details about what Charlie and Gwen are doing—how they are making out and how they are getting paid? How many miles they are running and what are the costs? I would have to talk to Charlie seriously to see what he thinks about the contract he signed, his expenses for the truck, and how he is coming out of it at the end of the month. I cannot afford to just go and lease a truck. I have financial responsibilities. I have my mother and brother to consider."

Ruth knew Dusty supported his family. That was why he worked so hard. He had been dedicated to helping his mother since the passing of his father. Ruth had met his family when they had been together and loved them all. His mother was an active member of the local community and volunteered her time in raising money for local charities. His brother lived at home and took the odd job here and there. They all liked Ruth, and Ruth always had a feeling of coming home when she went to visit.

Even during the times when Dusty's mother knew about both Ruth and Loretta, she and Ruth spent time discussing the situation. His mother had hoped Dusty would leave Loretta and establish a life with Ruth. Martha liked Ruth, what she stood for and how she and Dusty interacted.

She thought Ruth was good for Dusty and that Loretta's only goal was to drain him financially and use him as a meal ticket. Ruth agreed with her. Both women knew there was nothing they could do to open Dusty's eyes to the manipulation and control of Loretta.

Ruth had given up on Dusty ever leaving Loretta and had gone into trucking with a vengeance. She had moved forward in her life. She had completely stopped talking to him. The relationship was going nowhere as long as she was in the middle of his relationship with Loretta.

Ruth had analyzed her own feelings for Dusty and why she had put up with the way he treated her. She had to look long, hard, and deep inside herself to see he was another man in her life who made her feel unworthy and not enough. Her ex-husband had found other women throughout their marriage. Ruth ignored all those relationships because of the children.

The relationship she had before meeting Dusty had turned out the same. When Dusty came along a year and a half later, she was not looking, he just seemed to drop in out of nowhere, and they had clicked. She had let herself enjoy his company, and they had fun together, until the day Ruth found out he had a girlfriend and had not been completely upfront and honest with her. Then came the fights, the triggers for Ruth, and it only got worse as time went on. Ruth decided to let go before she ended up hating Dusty for the way he was treating her.

Ruth had spent far too many nights alone, unable to contact him, because he was with Loretta. She hated sitting in the truck alone while he went to make his nightly phone call to her. He texted her throughout the day, and as Ruth watched in silence, she started—one brick at a time—to build a wall of protection around her heart.

Ruth loved Dusty too much to sit back and watch the wonderful connection they had go the way of so many other unfaithful relationships. She got tired of trying to convince him that Loretta was only using him for her own purposes. So, Ruth made the decision to permanently make the break and move on.

Dusty had too many personal issues and seemed afraid to leave the relationship with Loretta. Ruth and Loretta were two totally different women. Ruth was fiercely independent. Loretta was extremely dependent. Ruth was outgoing, upbeat, and fun—a tomboy who flew by the seat of her pants.

Loretta was a stay-at-home mother who had an eighteen-year-old son living with her. Loretta did not want to work and did not try to improve her situation. She depended on Dusty for support. It was one of the reasons Ruth figured Dusty would not leave her. He felt responsible for Loretta and did not want to hurt her.

There were many times Ruth tried to leave, and more than once, she had advised Dusty not to contact her. Ruth knew the only way to win, or to feel good about herself, was to walk away from the situation. Dusty either loved her enough to follow or he did not. Ruth knew, if she stayed in the middle, there would be no decision made. There were two women, and Dusty could not make a choice; the women had to decide. Ruth knew, for her own sanity and well-being, she had to leave.

She had been right. According to Dusty, it was not long after Ruth withdrew from the three-way relationship that Loretta decided she could not trust Dusty. Loretta was continually wondering if he was lying to her and if he had actually broken off his relationship with Ruth. He had lied to her so many times about Ruth, she did not know what to believe and could no longer trust him.

Ruth had taken time to grieve the relationship, and then she had put all her efforts into working and driving. It was a good distraction, and she had just about put Dusty's memory to rest when they had reunited at the Aulac truck stop. Everything they felt for one another was rekindled and came rushing to the surface like a volcanic eruption. There was no stopping it, and there was no denying how they felt about one another.

Ruth talked to his mother from time to time, to see how he was doing. Martha relayed that he was doing fine, working too hard as usual, but that she still heard from him every day. She never mentioned to Ruth that Dusty and Loretta were no longer together.

Ruth was not interested in a long-term relationship, although she did miss the companionship of going out with a man. The other truckers steered clear of her, and she did not interact with anyone for fear that word might get back to Dusty. She did not want him thinking that all she wanted from him was the trucking industry and that she could so easily move on to another man.

Ruth was used to being alone and did not mind the solace and freedom to do what she pleased. Long ago, she had gotten used to eating out alone, going to movies alone, concerts, plays; anything and everything she wanted to do, she mainly did alone. People often wondered and worried about her travelling alone. She had the heart and soul of an adventurer.

CHAPTER 9
Living the Dream

Ruth enjoyed being alone, but it had cost her more than one date going further, and she had lost a lot of friends along the way. A lot of men did not like strong, independent women; they found them intimidating. Men had this mindset that only they were supposed to be the knight in shining armour and rescue the damsel in distress. Ruth was not one of those, and she thought she was hard to love.

When Ruth attended couples' functions alone, the women viewed her as a threat. They stood next to their men and watched as Ruth conversed with their husbands about hockey, trucking, NASCAR, and any other subject that went around in men's circles.

Ruth was so used to being and working in a man's world that topics such as makeup, hairstyles, fashion, and the latest fad diets did not interest her. She would much rather be involved in conversations about politics, sports, business, and the latest stock market news and real-estate trends.

Ruth was used to being shunned by the female population and intimidating to the male population. In Dusty, she had found a lighthearted, hardworking, real man who had old school values and who loved to have fun without any complications. All of these qualities had attracted Ruth. She opened herself up to him. As time went on, it seemed the more she opened up to him, the more he pulled away, until he swung back to Loretta like a boomerang.

Now, they were back together, both working hard. Yet, Ruth still had no idea where their relationship stood. One night, when they were in a truck stop curled up in her bunk, she decided to bring up the subject again.

"Dusty, I would like to talk to you about what you feel you want in a relationship with me now. I do not want to fight, and I do not want to get too heavily into it. I would like some direction from you as to where this may be going this time," she said in a soft voice.

Dusty coughed—he must have known the subject would come up eventually. He took her in his arms. "Look, Ruth, we have been together for a long time now, you may as well say. We both realize this is what we want. Unfortunately, by the time I realized you were what I wanted, you had disappeared. When I could not talk to you or get a hold of you, I realized how much I missed having you in my life. I tried to bury my feelings for you and move forward, but it felt like I had died. I could not seem to get past you. I thought about where you might be, what you were doing, whether you were seeing anyone, and what an idiot I had been for letting you go. I am not going to make the same mistake again. I want us to be together, no matter where that may be. If that means only seeing you from truck stop to truck stop for the time being, or we are driving team in our own truck, it doesn't matter to me. All I want is to be where you are, and for you to be where I am. How we make that work, we will have to figure out. I love you, and I want to be with you."

Ruth could feel the tears well up in her eyes. She could not believe her ears. After all they had been through over almost two years in which she had known him, he had finally come to the conclusion he was ready to enter into a full-time, committed relationship with her. Ruth took Dusty's head in her hands and looked him in the eyes.

"I have waited a long time for you to say those words. I love you, too. Looks like destiny is finally starting to work in our favour. I knew you came into my life for a reason the day I met you, and I knew you were here to stay. You make me so happy."

Ruth and Dusty started asking their dispatchers to move them in the same direction, which gave them more time to be together on the road. Ruth did not want to leave Nationwide Transport, but she was beginning to resent having to be away from Dusty. The company Dusty worked for was not interested in hiring Ruth. They were downsizing, and taking on a new driver was not something they wanted to get into. New drivers were expensive on their insurance, and they were already going through a restructuring because of an accident where one of their trucks had been written off. The insurance cost for the accident would have been astronomical, and Ruth was wondering if the result of the accident was hitting their bottom line.

Ruth looked into all the details of owning her own truck and the different ways it could be achieved. She had already been pre-approved to lease a truck that was well within her means. She looked at companies that leased. They provided the loads, insurance, and a lot of different fees that were very expensive for anyone trying to get started.

The only thing Ruth was up against was that she was a new driver. She mentioned this to Dusty and approached him about becoming the primary driver, until she reached the time where she would be able to take over the lease herself. He had been somewhat receptive to the idea when he was still with Loretta.

Ruth had decided to back off from the idea. She knew how Loretta sat home, did nothing, and expected Dusty to support her, in addition to helping his own family. He worked his backside off to make money so he could afford the two households. Ruth would not contribute to Loretta staying home.

Ruth had grown up working hard. She knew what it meant to go out and forge a financial life for herself. She could hustle, and it was one of the reasons the entertainers liked working with her. When Ruth sunk her teeth into something, she was like a dog with a bone. She was all in.

When she was married, she worked at whatever she could, wherever she could, to help support the family. Ruth knew what tough times were. She refused to seek help from local charities—too proud to accept it. She had taken out her pencil, hunkered down, and figured out a budget, and she had stuck to it.

Ruth had ditched the idea of leasing a truck for her and Dusty to go on the road together like Charlie and Gwen. She decided to take a job on her own and see what happened from there. It had not been too bad so far. Ruth knew in her heart she and Dusty could make a go of it, if only he did not have Loretta as an albatross around his neck.

Ruth supported Dusty in helping to support his mother and brother. Family was family. They depended on him to help make ends meet, and to handle whatever financial surprise popped up. When it came to Loretta treating Dusty like her meal ticket and taking advantage of his hard work, Ruth would have no part in it.

Once Ruth had established that she and Dusty were on a strong relationship footing, felt comfortable looking into leasing a truck from the same company Charlie and Gwen were leasing theirs. There were so many factors that had to be taken into consideration. Ruth was determined to learn the industry and to see if they could live off the proceeds while leasing their own truck. It would be a beginning. Once they had a year or two under their belt, maybe they could lease another one, and then another one, and hire drivers to drive them. It could be the beginning of their own small fleet and a healthy nest egg for them to retire on.

Insurance was her biggest concern, and trying to find the loads herself. There were many downfalls to that avenue, but Ruth was willing to look at it. Being an owner–operator was a big risk, and one Ruth was not willing to take. She could lease a truck like Charlie and Gwen, and if that did not work out, the truck could go back to the company and she could call it a day.

Abby and Ambrose put in their opinions when Ruth mentioned she wanted to lease or lease-to-own her own truck. They were worried she was throwing her money away. Ruth assured them the truck would be leased under a company name. Therefore, her personal financial status would not be affected, should things not go well.

Ambrose was the financial guru of the family. He was always there with financial advice for his mother when he thought she needed it. His main concern was her getting tangled up with someone who would strip her of her inheritance and leave her with nothing.

Ruth was careful not to introduce Dusty to her children. Abby had her own ideas about her mother dating, and it always caused a ripple in their relationship. Ambrose was very protective of Ruth and saw every man as a potential threat to his mother's financial status. Men had a way of waltzing lonely women with money down the garden path. Ambrose did not want to see his mother end up with nothing because a man had taken advantage of her.

Ruth knew Ambrose had concerns and she was careful. She had a girlfriend who had unexpectedly become a widow and had come into a substantial amount of money. Less than a year later, she remarried. In six months, she was broke and declaring bankruptcy. The man had beaten her, spent her money, and disappeared.

Ruth saw this possibly happening again with her friend Cindy. Cindy had gotten tangled up with a man, following the death of her husband. He drank excessively and spent most of his time in the basement. She had run her own business for over thirty years, and she had decided to sell and retire. The sale would bring her a substantial amount of money. Ruth was worried for Cindy that the same thing would happen to her, once the sale of the business went through.

Cindy had been happy for Ruth when she met Dusty, but, after a while, Cindy refused to believe Dusty would leave Loretta, like he said he would. Cindy had been married to a trucker in her first marriage. He had cheated on her. She let that experience cloud her when making friends with Dusty. Cindy had grown tired of the situation between Ruth and Dusty, and had decided Ruth enjoyed the relationship. Cindy did not approve of Ruth running around with a man who was already in a relationship.

Ruth had lost a lot of friends when she went into the trucking industry and started driving. There were those who thought she was crazy, and it was just another fun thing for Ruth to do. These were people who saw Ruth as a free spirit who was never able to settle down. Most people did not understand Ruth's longing to travel the way she did.

They seemed to think Ruth was missing something in her life, and continually searching for something she could not find. They felt sorry for her and hoped one day she would find the person or place she was looking for. They could not accept this was who Ruth was, and that she really enjoyed the lifestyle she led. Ruth used to shake her head, and after a while, their opinions did not matter any longer. She went her own way, and slowly those people had let themselves out of Ruth's life.

Over the summer, Ruth and her children were all together for the funeral and to clean out the house. It was a bittersweet reunion. There was so much work to do, but as it turned out, it was easier than they expected. They laughed and cried about the memories the house contained for each of them. Abby had the hardest time, but with Caleb there, it made it easier for her.

They boxed everything they wanted to keep and hauled it to a storage unit. Ruth put an advertisement in the local paper and had an open house flea market, as planned. The children did not want to be around for it, so they packed up a picnic lunch and went to the beach for the day.

People came and went, and before long the house was empty. The rest was hauled away by a local junk dealer. The real-estate agent had the house sold. It was in an excellent location and was a beautiful family home on a well-manicured lot. As soon as the agent knew it was going to be up for sale, she had the perfect couple waiting to purchase it and move in.

Now that everything was complete, Abby could go home, Ambrose was free of the responsibility of looking after the place, and Ruth could go back on the road.

She was starting to find out who her friends were. Those who stayed in touch knew she would get back to them whenever she could. There were others who thought even when she was on the road she should be in constant contact. They needed someone to unload their problems on. Ruth found, after these conversations, that she was drained and concerned about their situations. This affected her driving, and ability to concentrate on the road. She started returning their calls when she was on reset and did not have any further driving to do.

Ruth enjoyed her reset times. For every seventy hours of driving, she had to take thirty-six hours off. It was the law. So, wherever she was, she would shut down and relax. Her mind occasionally wandered to Gabe and how he used to spend his down time. Ruth had done the same thing and stopped somewhere away from the truck stops. She did not mind being parked in provincial or state visitor centre parking lots and tourist pull overs. There were trails she could walk, and fire pits, and she did not mind being alone. Ruth was never nervous or scared about travelling alone. The more she did it, the more she wanted to do it. She felt safe in her truck, always took the necessary precautions, and tried to stay aware of what was going on around her.

The truck stops were busy. Big rigs were coming and going all night. TriPacs and engines were running all night. Ruth was used to the white noise of the truck stop parking lots, but she did not feel as safe there. There were too many men hovering around when she went inside, and some of the looks she received were not welcoming. There had been more than one woman assaulted in a truck stop parking lot. There was so much noise that a screaming woman being dragged between parked trailers in the dark would never be heard.

Ruth knew it was a male-dominated industry. She had gotten many unwanted advances. Their remarks were degrading and vile in some cases. Others were nice and supportive of her choice of careers, but she still stayed away. Having a man in her life was not something she needed or wanted.

Ruth was a loner. She was happy in her truck, going down the road, and doing what she wanted to do. She did not need a man to feel fulfilled. She knew a lot of women who did, and who could not live without a man in their life. It was all they talked about, whether it was good or bad. It was either, how great he was or what an asshole he was. Ruth listened and took it all in, without making any comments.

Ruth missed Dusty, but knew it was the best thing she could have done for herself. He was so indecisive, and it was going nowhere. She had chalked it up to a lesson learned and moved on. If he was meant for her, he would come back; if he was not, then she would never see him again. Ruth believed destiny had played a huge part in their first meeting and in their reunion; she was willing to see how far it would go.

CHAPTER 10
Coming Home

The winter months were coming fast, and Ruth started to wonder whether she wanted to face another winter behind the wheel. The first year had been a scary one for her. She respected the machine she drove. She knew the damage it could do if she lost control and hit another vehicle.

She had to slow down and drive extremely carefully. As she had told Dusty, some of the driving conditions the previous winter were white knuckle for her. She only lost control once or twice during the icy stretches, and that was enough. Close calls were good; some of her trucker friends had not been so lucky and ended up in the ditch, or worse. After much consideration, Ruth decided that she would drive for the winter, at least until the time came when she knew where her relationship with Dusty was going.

Dusty and Ruth continued to talk about getting their own truck and running team. He still seemed to be reluctant to the idea, and she did not bring it up much. Ruth was beginning to think Dusty was still indecisive as to what he wanted to do.

Neither one of them talked about their relationship going to the next level, him moving his stuff from his mother's place to her place, or them co-habitating. This time, Ruth was not going to let herself jump whole-heartedly back into the same type of wishy-washy relationship they had before.

If Dusty was unable to commit to her, even after Loretta kicked him out, then she was not going to push the matter and would accept their relationship for what it was: two people enjoying each other's company whenever their paths crossed.

Ruth decided to take the leasing of a truck further, but decided she was not going to be the one to drive it over the winter months. She had signed the paperwork on a W900 Kenworth, and Andrew, a long-time childhood friend, was driving it for her. It seemed to be working well for both of them. She did not mention the business deal she had with Andrew to Dusty. She wanted to keep that to herself.

Andrew and Ruth had decided that he would take the truck out West and work the oil patches in Alberta, and he was making good money doing it—as much as fifteen thousand a month hauling fuel. It was going well. There was more than enough for Andrew to support himself, to pay the expenses of the truck, and for Ruth to pocket some money, too. It was a win–win situation for both of them.

Before Ruth knew it, she was well into the holidays again. Dusty was home with his mother and family for Christmas, and Ruth was on the road. The holidays really did not mean much to Ruth now that her children were grown up and had left home. She used to decorate extensively. When the children were small, her house looked like Santa's Workshop. She had collected almost three hundred nutcrackers over the years, had four Christmas trees, and every nook and cranny of the house seemed to have a Christmas decoration in it.

She did not mind being alone during the holidays, though some people did. To Ruth it was just another day in the world of a trucker. Her sister wanted her to come and spend Christmas with her, but Ruth refused. She could not depend on the weather, and she did not want to get stranded and unable to get back to her truck, should the weather and roads close.

She opted to take a load before Christmas down south to the United States. There were so many truckers who wanted to be home with their families and children for the holidays, Ruth did not mind working while they took the time off. Freight still had to move, no matter what the day, so Ruth concentrated on moving it for the guys who wanted to be home.

Dusty and Ruth continued to meet up when their schedules allowed and enjoyed each time they got together. Dusty often questioned Ruth about her travels, who she met up with, what she was doing, and Ruth often thought he did not trust her. She told him the truth and decided he would either believe her or not believe her, there was nothing she could do about it.

The winter months passed. Andrew had approached her about getting an additional truck, increasing their fleet to two trucks and putting another one in the oil patch. Ruth agreed, and their second truck came on board in early February. At the rate they were going, Ruth thought by the end of the year, they could very possibly be up to four trucks.

Ruth looked at leasing a third truck in March just to haul freight. She was getting pretty good at how to hustle for a load, and decided it might be time to take the risk and expand a bit faster than she and Andrew had originally planned. She decided to go ahead on her own, without consulting Andrew, and lease another truck.

Ruth left Nationwide Transport when she leased the third truck, and she had all kinds of time to sit at the computer and search for loads for her trucks. She watched who was hiring owner–operators and how their systems worked. She dreamed of owning her own company, and that was exactly where she was concentrating her efforts.

Business was booming. She had three semis in service and three drivers. She approached Dusty and told him she was considering leasing an additional truck through the same company Charlie and Gwen were driving for. Dusty had been receptive to the idea, in theory, but he still seemed reluctant to take a leap of faith.

Charlie and Gwen were making good money through the company they worked with. Ruth could see no reason not to lease a truck there. Dusty would be behind the wheel, and the company would be finding the freight and covering some of the costliest expenses. There was money to be made, and Ruth would have a fourth truck on the road by the beginning of the summer.

Ruth's bank account was growing. She needed very little to live on. She had long-since become a person who only bought what she needed, not what she wanted. She had made some significant purchases over the years, to spoil herself, but she was very conscious of her financial procurements and didn't waste money needlessly.

It was spring, and Ruth looked around her little apartment in Sydney. It was time to give it up and find a place where she could work the company and have a stable for Waylon. She dreamed of a little spot next to the ocean, where she could work and have a view overlooking the water.

She started looking at real estate in Dusty's hometown. It was a lovely little town and she had fallen in love with it the first time she had gone there to visit. It was a bit larger than most of the small fishing villages along the coast of Newfoundland. She liked the atmosphere of small towns and the down-home folks who were full of life, laughter, song, and love.

Ruth had been welcomed with open arms by Dusty's mother when they first met. They had hit it off right from the beginning. Martha was impressed with Ruth and the way she pampered Dusty, and she liked that Ruth was not involved with him for support, the way Loretta had been. Martha had never been fond of Loretta and had found her a drain on Dusty. Ruth had met Dusty's brother and found it hard to understand his heavy Newfoundland accent most of the time, but she found him as witty and fun as Dusty.

One night, Ruth and Dusty were curled up in the bunk of his truck. Dusty had returned to his mother's after being on the road for an extended period of time. Ruth missed being on the road with him, but was happy in her little apartment in Sydney for the time being, while running the company. She had taken the trip to Newfoundland with him to see his mother, and they had all had a pleasant evening.

"Dusty, we need to talk. I need to know what your plans are for the future. I have been thinking about giving up the apartment and buying a small piece of property with a little house and enough pasture for Waylon to graze. I have thought about a second horse for you, too, if you want one. We could ride together, when you are home. I am thinking it might be time for me to settle down. I am interested in your thoughts and what you may feel you might want to do?"

Ruth figured it was time to tell Dusty about the small fleet she had on the road, and that business was booming. She never wanted a large fleet, and, with the prospect of Dusty driving a fourth truck in the fleet, things could only get better. She liked the idea of leasing from the same company Charlie and Gwen were leasing. There was no money down, they found the loads, and Charlie and Gwen seemed to be happy with them.

Dusty was surprised she had already gone ahead with the company. He knew she was set on it, but he did not think she would go ahead without him. He listened intently to what she had to say. She was smart and had picked up a lot in the short time she had been driving a truck and involved in the industry. She had taken the opportunity to study how things worked, to learn about the trucks, and what the expenses would be in owning one. She had a vision when it came to what she wanted to do, and she had followed through with it.

Dusty seemed impressed with all she told him. He was not crazy about her working with Andrew, but she had made it work to their advantage by having Andrew put, and manage, the trucks in the oil patch. Andrew was knowledgeable and knew what needed to be done. He obviously had a good handle on things as they already had two trucks there. Ruth told Dusty about the other one she had put on the road about a month before, and that she was dispatching it herself. It was doing well, and she was more than ready to lease another truck for Dusty to drive to enhance the fleet.

Dusty could not believe how fast Ruth was putting trucks on the road, and how things were working out for her. She was a worker; he knew, when she put her mind to it and buckled down, she was one to get things done. When she got started on something, she made things happen.

"I will have to think about it. I am not one to jump in the way you do."

"Well, let me know soon, because I would love to have you in a truck driving down the road for us. As you can see, things are going well, and in less than a year, I have three trucks on the road. So, I am excited about the possibilities of having another one with you behind the wheel. Now, what about buying a place? What do you think of that? I would like to get started on something soon. It is late April and a good time to make a decision, find something suitable, and move. It will be easier to move Waylon in the summer months, too."

"I think you getting a place is a great idea. I think it is time we look at moving in together and start moving forward."

Ruth smiled, "Okay then, let's start looking at something that is suitable. I know what I want. A little place on the water. I do not need much. There should be something around the area we can make ours."

"Whatever you want. I will be happy wherever you are. Now, I think, it is time we get some sleep. We both have an early start in the morning."

Ruth rolled over and they both assumed their normal sleeping positions. Ruth smiled at how his backside seemed to fit perfectly into the curve in the small of her back. It was like a human heating pad after a long, hard day and made her back feel so much better in the morning.

They pulled away from his mother's driveway. The sun was shining, and Ruth felt like her life was finally coming together. She would have a small trucking fleet of four trucks, and Dusty would soon be driving one of them. She was happy he was going to leave R.A.E. and become involved with her company.

Andrew was disappointed when Ruth told him she and Dusty were back together, and she had gone ahead and leased a couple of trucks on her own and that Dusty was going to drive one of them. Andrew had always had a soft spot in his heart for Ruth and had hoped it might develop into much more over time. He told her he had recognized her business savvy a few years before and regretted not pursuing her as a partner back then.

Ruth was full of life and had an energy about her that was infectious. She was upbeat, never let anything get her down, and when she was focused, she went forward with a diligence that was pretty much unheard of. She never wavered from her end goal, whatever it was, and always seemed to come out on top, no matter what she put her mind to.

Ruth's bank account continued to grow, and her longing for a little place to settle down in, to work at getting loads for her trucks, and to spend the days doing whatever she wanted was calling her. Ruth had been a gypsy over the past ten years, and she could feel herself wanting, more and more, to get off the road and maybe even retire from driving.

Dusty had a piece of property, but Ruth was not sure about moving there. There were two houses on the property, and his mother and brother lived in one. He said the other house should be torn down and a new place built, but Ruth had never been in the house. She had been to his home a couple of times to visit his family, but he had never shown her the other house.

Ruth started looking at real estate in the area and came across a unique houseboat-style house on a cliff, with a couple of acres. It had a bow as the front deck, built overlooking the ocean. It had everything she needed, and it was definitely within her price range. She called the realtor and went and took a look at it. From the minute she walked through the door, she knew it was where she wanted to be. She told the realtor to draw up the paperwork.

Ruth could not wait to move in and make it her own. There was little that had to be changed, and she knew those things would come in time. She hired a local contractor to erect a suitable size barn for two horses and was anxious to have it completed so she could move the horses and get settled in their new home.

When Dusty heard what Ruth had done, he was thrilled. "That's awesome news. I know the property, and it is a great little spot. One thing, though, I was thinking, why don't we buy Scooter and move him with Waylon? We could ride together, and the two of them would not have to be separated."

"That's a great idea. I will contact the owner and see if she is interested in selling him. I do not see why she would not—she never visits him."

Ruth hung up the phone and called the stable to get the contact information for Scooter's owner. It wasn't long before Ruth was making a deal over the phone for Scooter and settling the matter of e-transferring the money to her. When the deal was complete and arrangements had been made for the bill of sale, Ruth called Dusty back to tell him he now owned a horse.

"I will transfer the money to you," Dusty said.

"Don't bother. He is my gift to you," Ruth replied.

Things were moving along so swiftly; Ruth could hardly keep up. She had moved into her house and the trucks she had on the road were making money, life was good for both of them. Ruth loved living in the little town, and was beginning to make friends fast. She spent her days working on securing loads for the trucks, and, in her spare time, she rode horseback and took part in community events with Dusty's mother. Life was simple there, uncomplicated, and Ruth thought she had finally found a place where she could take her boots off, kick up her feet, and put down some roots.

Dusty stayed on the road with the fourth truck. He was home as much as he could be and missed Ruth travelling with him. "Why don't you come out on the road with me again for a while. I miss you being out here with me," he said one night on the phone.

Ruth agreed; she too missed the road, and the next time Dusty came home, she had her bags packed and they pulled out of the driveway together. It was like old times. They laughed, sang together, and had fun. They lived a quiet life, and Ruth relished in it.

When they returned from the road and a visit with the family, Dusty and Ruth sat on the deck of their little house having a drink. It was a beautiful evening. The wind was cool, and they sat, cuddled together on the porch swing, bundled up in blankets. They had a small fire burning in the outdoor firepit, and the air was crisp. Ruth adored the weather in Newfoundland. It was usually wild and windy. It was a beautiful night, and the moon was starting to rise over the bay.

"I never imagined life could be so wonderful. You have made such a difference in my life. We have been through a lot together, and I think it is time to solidify our relationship," Dusty said, looking at her with love in his eyes.

Dusty stood up in front of Ruth and bent down on one knee, pulling a small green velvet box from his pocket. "Marry me, Ruth. Make me the happiest man in the world by becoming my wife," he said, looking up at her. Ruth looked at the small, delicate emerald nestled in the setting of an engraved Celtic band.

She was astonished by Dusty's proposal of marriage. It was something she vowed she would never do again. But, as she looked at him, a huge smile came across her face, "You have just made me the happiest woman in the world. Of course, I will be your wife."

Dusty slipped the little ring on her finger as he stood up in front of her. Ruth raised herself from the chair to hug and kiss the man she had been madly in love with for so long.

Dusty turned her around, put his arm around her, and they both stood on the deck of their house built like a boat and watched the moon rise over the bay.

Ruth could not help but think, she was finally home.

ABOUT THE AUTHOR

ANGEL POWER is an adventurer and has traveled extensively in Canada, the United States and Europe. A former
Event Coordinator in the entertainment industry she has
worked with some of Canada's top professional entertainers
and has lived in a variety of cities and rural areas across the
country. She has been published in numerous newspapers
and magazines and is a firm believer in living life to the
fullest and following your dreams. The Mother of two, she
spends her time on the road travelling, horseback riding,
hiking and doing genealogy. She presently makes her home
in Nova Scotia, where she is working on a new novel.

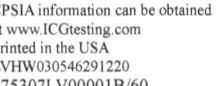
CPSIA information can be obtained
at www.ICGtesting.com
Printed in the USA
LVHW030546291220
675307LV00001B/60

9 781525 579691